DARKWALKER 4
ARMAGEDDON

This is a work of fiction.
Similarities to persons, living or dead,
are neither intended
nor should be inferred.

ISBN: 0-9983882-8-9
ISBN-13: 978-0-9983882-8-1 (DarkFluidity)

ALSO BY JOHN URBANCIK

NOVELS
Sins of Blood and Stone
Breath of the Moon
Once Upon a Time in Midnight
Stale Reality
The Corpse and the Girl from Miami
DarkWalker 1: Hunting Grounds
DarkWalker 2: Inferno
DarkWalker 3: The Deep City

NOVELLAS
A Game of Colors
The Rise and Fall of Babylon (with Brian Keene)
Wings of the Butterfly
House of Shadow and Ash
Necropolis
Quicksilver
Beneath Midnight
Zombies vs. Aliens vs. Robots vs. Cowboys vs. Ninja vs.
Investment Bankers vs. Green Berets
Colette and the Tiger

COLLECTIONS
Shadows, Legends & Secrets
Sound and Vision
Tales of the Fantastic and the Phantasmagoric

INKSTAINS
Multiple volumes

DARKWALKER 4
ARMAGEDDON

JOHN URBANCIK

PART ONE
VERMILLION

CHAPTER ONE

1.

The night air is brisk, so Colton crowds close to his little fire and rubs his hands over the flames. He hasn't washed. The stink comes off him waves. The crusted dirt on his skin hides crusted blood. He pauses with his hands, to take a swig from his flask. He hasn't gone far. He's unfamiliar with the world above. He hasn't seen stars for most of a lifetime, or felt real winds, and he knows he won't long survive out here.

He keeps his back to the mountains and the forests. He's concerned only with what will emerge from the mouth of this cave. It's not much of a mouth, just a hole, a crack between rocks. He's no good with directions or he might've gone down to the deep city himself. But he was never part of that place. They wouldn't have accepted him. They'd have combed through his flesh and peeled back his soul in layers. He was never prepared for that.

He's not prepared for the DarkWalker, either, but Jack Harlow emerges and looks at him and grins a wicked sort of grin. "*Warlock.*"

"I escaped," Colton says, still crouched over the fire. "I thought you might like to share some fire, some water." He offers his flask. "Kentucky bourbon."

The DarkWalker looks at him with changed eyes, with a hint of vicious intent. Colton knows he's not the intended target, but much has changed since he last saw the DarkWalker in that sham of a shallow city, that stage play enacted at the highest levels of the city, the seer's little farce. Just the thought of her, he spits into the fire. The flames dance.

"Tell me what happened," the DarkWalker says.

"What you expected, I imagine," the warlock says. "There ain't much more to tell than that. They brought down the mine, they brought down the shallow city. Nothing left of Silver Blade."

"The mining town is still here."

"Overrun. I wouldn't get close."

"I will." The DarkWalker speaks with a confidence he never had before. He'd been cocky, sure, and maybe arrogant, but there's depth and consequence now.

"The seer and her sister, they enlisted, entangled, and ensnared armies to fight." Armies is too big a word, but any other word would be too small. "That brought the watchers. They only wanted to escape. There are – there *were* fortifications I ain't got much know of. They discarded me as merely a man with tricks."

The DarkWalker smiles, because the DarkWalker knows exactly what that means.

"The watchers came, and they brought destruction, but it was your *woman* – your so-called friend, who released the magic and sparked the flame to bring the whole thing down."

"They've got her now," the DarkWalker says.

"The mine swallowed a lot. That don't mean much."

The DarkWalker shakes his head. "I don't care."

"Silver Blade was meant to be a prison," the warlock says.

The DarkWalker grins again. It's a hungry expression. "I know." He brandishes the pendant the warlock had given him before the mine collapsed. "Does this do what I think it does?"

"Probably not," Colton says. "What do you think it does?"

"I think it'll guide me."

"It's a guide of some sort. But not here. Save it for another day. Have you got a plan, or at least an intention?"

"First," the DarkWalker tells him, "I'm going to rescue Naomi."

The warlock waits for the DarkWalker to continue.

"Then I'm going to destroy them."

"You'll need help."

"You're free because of me," the DarkWalker says. "I assume that means you owe me a debt."

With reluctance, Colton admits, "It does."

The DarkWalker grins again. "Just how strong is your magic, warlock?"

He returns the grin. "Call me Colton."

2.

Dawn approaches, but the clouds obscure it. A storm gathers around the old mining town. Silver Blade must feel it. Colton feels it, certainly, and even the DarkWalker seems affected. The storm's been gathering for nine days, since the shallow city fell. It swallows the smoke venting through holes in the ground. The insides of the mountain, of the mine, seem still to be settling, but there's a good chance fire still rages underground. There was something natural about that fire, but something unnatural as well – something magical and something supernatural, a mixture of ingredients the warlock will never comprehend.

The DarkWalker asks, "Who or what else escaped?"

"That I saw," Colton says, "only a few spirits who were able to slip through the cracks. Anything that tried to get out of the mine, the watchers were there waiting for them."

"To kill or capture?"

"A little of both?" Colton shakes his head once. "I don't really know."

The DarkWalker sits across from Colton, on the rock he'd moved there. He looks up to the sky, the clouds, as though he can see the stars through them. "Why were you waiting for me?"

Colton takes a breath. He doesn't know how to say this. "I'm just a man." When the DarkWalker says nothing, he goes on. "I might've been something. Done something. Who can say? But they sent me into the mines instead."

"The watchers?"

"I'm an old man," Colton says. "Everything hurts.

Especially the echoes of what never was." He takes a breath. "I want justice."

"Vengeance," the DarkWalker says.

Colton shrugs. "Either. Doesn't matter. I've always known one thing, DarkWalker, one thing that's made all the difference in my life, which made all the years under the mines so goddamn horrible."

"What's that?"

"I know the date I die."

For a moment, Colton's lost in his head, in his memories, the caverns and the creatures, the blood, the darkness, the ascension from one level to the next. He'd never believed it would end. There'd always be more caves, more mines, more beasts and ghouls. He never thought he'd see the stars again. The moon.

And even now, they hide behind these clouds.

The DarkWalker breaks the silence. "My name's Jack Harlow."

3.

Through the night, the DarkWalker sits. He acknowledges the arrivals as they come. The first is a spirit, a wisp of a thing, drifting like smoke with a vaguely feminine shape. She settles between the shadows thrown by the fire, seems to meet Jack Harlow's eyes, and makes no sound. In all his life in the mines, Colton never saw anything like her.

A brick of a man, not more than four feet tall but nearly as broad, skin like marbleized granite and eyes like curdled milk grunts when he sees the DarkWalker sitting there and says, "Fuck it all." He glances at Colton and says, "Fuck you too." Then he holds his hands over the fire and says, one last time, almost under his breath, "*Fuck.*"

Next, a hunched, scaly beast incapable of speech. It snarls and spills saliva from its teeth, of which it has plenty. It reminds Colton of a dog and a frog, or his memory of a frog, which goes back so far he doesn't know how to count the years. It looks hungry. It looks like hunger. It nuzzles next to the DarkWalker, who casually lowers a hand to scratch the back of its neck.

A girl comes next, one of the upper level servants of the seer. She still wears her jewels, some of her jewels, though her clothes are torn and dirty. She stinks as bad as Colton and she's covered with old scars, fresh cuts and smudged ash. When she sees the DarkWalker, her eyes get big and white. He just looks back at her for a long time. Finally, she says, "I don't know how I'm here."

"Neither do I," Jack Harlow tells her.

"I thought the fire would consume me."

When the DarkWalker doesn't answer that, Colton says, "I thought the fire would consume everything."

"What of your master?" Jack Harlow asks her.

"The seer," the girl says, bowing her head. "It was horrible. The fire, there was so much of it, spreading through the air like tendrils, like living things. The flames burrowed into her and lit up her veins so that she was just like her sister. She burned from the inside out. It was..." She takes a breath, and concludes with the only word she still knows. "Horrible."

"You're useless to me," Jack Harlow tells her.

The girl's face drops. Like she's just been rejected for a job, by a lover, by her personal god. She stammers. "I – I have skills."

Jack Harlow turns away from her and stares into the fire.

"Are you punishing me?"

He doesn't answer.

She runs to his side, kneels besides him, clings to his arm and shoulder. "I was The Lady's property," she says, pleading, pulling at him, but would have better luck trying to budge a locomotive half buried in mud. She's sobbing, taking gulps of breath. "I didn't have a choice then and I still don't now."

The DarkWalker turns his eyes on the girl. There's depth in those eyes that Colton never saw when the DarkWalker first arrived in the shallow city. Then, Colton might have been able to guess what would happen next. Underground, such displays of weakness, of dependency, were rare, but Jack Harlow had been a rarity in the darkness. Now, he was as much darkness as not, and he might just as easily kill her as take her for a concubine.

Tenderly, he touches her chin, raises her face so she can look up to him. Colton feels himself leaning closer to get a better look across the fire. He barely hears Jack Harlow whisper to her. "Your life is your own again. If you stay with me, you will die, and I don't wish that for you."

They hold that pose too long. Colton grows uncomfortable and glances at the others. More have arrived, some wounded and some barely substantial. The DarkWalker ignores all of them, instead focusing on the fragile human girl. She gets control of her voice. "I am beyond any other hope."

The DarkWalker nods. He lets go of her face, and says nothing more to her. Dawn is coming. The DarkWalker surveys the band of them, not more than a dozen, and says, "This is a rescue. None of you matter to me. I will sacrifice any and all of you to save my friend. I promise nothing, except – if any of you get in my way or somehow prevent me from accomplishing my goal, I will destroy you utterly."

As far as motivational speeches go, it seems effective.

4.

Beau grumbles and growls. There's no target, it's just the sounds he makes, and he makes them despite the extraordinary taste of fresh air. It's been a long time, too long, and though it's true he's always lived within a mountain, no one knows better than he the difference between natural caves and the mines carved by the hands of men.

He sneers at the thought.

He can never go back home. Home *was* an ocean away, but the men who took him, so many years ago, collapsed those tunnels and stole the treasures he'd spent most of a century protecting. Human men. Mortal men. He did some damage, yes, and even now the thought makes him smile. He knows how his smiles look.

He rises. Movement takes effort. Time has taken its toll on him. His bones ache. Most of the past decades, he'd been content to burrow deeper, to pass the time, to sleep. He doesn't recognize the creatures around him, except of course the DarkWalker. He doesn't care for any of them.

Death. The DarkWalker offers it, but doesn't demand it. Beaumont Laurent has never followed anyone before. He's never had the need. But now, the DarkWalker's intentions align with his own. The men who had defeated him, the men who condemned him to this place, may still live. And if not them, the men who have taken their place, the same organization, the same *terrible* humans. It'll feel good to squeeze their skulls and crack their necks.

"Gnome," the DarkWalker says, looking at him. "Are you with me?"

Beau takes a breath. He considers his words. He says, "Fuck, I guess I am."

5.

In ages unknown, undreamt by modern man and unremembered, the three Sisters of Shadow crept into existence, born of shadow and moonlight and desire. They were beauties in an age before beauty. And the youngest of them, the fairest and sharpest and most dangerous, slipped through the ages taking lovers and children and gifts and blood. As her strength increases, she taught her sisters the ways of shadow and ash, and she tempted the gods, and she learned to corrode and consume souls.

How much of their history is true? Even the Sisters of Shadow don't know. They're not bound by memory or truth or anything. The legends about them have shifted and changed and dissipated, and it's possible they never came into existence at all.

But Sibyl, as she's been called, certainly seems to exist, and she gathers under the DarkWalker because among the things she does remember, among the clearest and most precise of those memories, is that a DarkWalker was old when the Sisters were born. She may owe no allegiance to this particular DarkWalker, but there's a history, and there's a debt.

She takes his hand and conveys to him certain facts. Her name, Sibyl, which she acquired not too many hundreds of years before. Her intentions: to fight for the DarkWalker in an attempt to recover his lost lover. She and her Sisters know of love.

Ah, but this isn't a lover. After countless ages and eras and eons, the DarkWalker surprises her. Not rescuing a lover in the traditional sense, in the ways of flesh and passion – there was another, now lost, a creature called Sparrow.

Sibyl removes her hand. She's given and taken. It's enough. She sees the discord in his shadow, the tumult, the anger. And also the love. And echoes of Shadow, which Sibyl knows so well.

Their connection is tenuous and brief, but she reassures him. Theirs is not an impossible task. He could do it alone, but he doesn't have to and he won't. These creatures around him will die for him, most of them, because they see him as some sort of savoir. It's untrue and unsavory. She lets him know he's not the savior, but the one who needs saving. Even her allies, she haunts.

6.

The beast follows her new master. He is a strange one, and his hand is a comfort. She isn't accustomed to comforts of any sort. The occasional bit of raw meat, sure. The warmth and safety of a lair or a pit or a cage. She has seen much. She has outlived masters. She has devoured masters, and she knows from experience they are sour and bitter and not good eating, but sometimes satisfying nonetheless.

Her name is and has always been *Rana*, because when her first master made her, when the good doctor had conjoined the pieces of flesh and stole a spark of innocence, the cries and tears and blood of an infant, there had been amphibians and tadpoles and toads and frogs.

Rana knows these things even if she doesn't know them. She remembers the scent of the good doctor, and she remembers all the things he ever said and did and gave her, but she'd never understood it all. Fire, bad. She got that. And she got plenty of fresh meat. The good doctor was always incredibly good at that. If she thinks too much about him, she misses him, but only because he had made her and he had been good to her and she had eaten his corpse before escaping the laboratory.

Not all of her masters have been so kind.

This new master, this master she's chosen herself, this master who had saved her from the depths, he is good but not as good as the doctor. He won't feed her like the doctor had fed her. He won't love her as the doctor had loved her. But also, he won't beat her, and he won't lie to her. She is old. She's very old. She understands death because a part of her had been born from humanity. She doesn't have words, and she doesn't think in words, but she understands concepts and possibilities, and she understands fate, and she recognizes the scents of vengeance.

7.

Dawn rises over the city of Silver Blade. It's a stretch, calling it a city. It might have been once, when the silver mine was operating, but that was a long time ago and no mortal alive remembers those days.

The men in the city now walk in patrols, two together, heavily armed. Their instructions are to clean the streets, and each believes what they're doing is justified. They've seen the filmstrips and videotapes of some of these creatures in full rampage. They're armed with specialized bullets incorporating a number of metals and alloys dangerous to the creatures of the night. Armor piercing, hollow point, explosive, tainted with various poisons and elixirs. They take this kind of job because they have faith in the organization they work for.

They are all, essentially, soldiers. Mercenaries. They follow orders and collect their pay – good chunks of money and a nice retirement package – but they are only soldiers. Expendable.

All of them have seen photographs of the DarkWalker. Their instructions in his regard are explicit. At the Fox and Silver Sparrow, Lance Turner waves over another drink. Brina, the old woman who runs the joint, brings him a stein full of something thick and amber. "I ain't your damned servant," she tells him. The drink sloshes as she bangs it down in front of him.

He grins at her. He says, "I'll be gone soon enough."

"Yeah, I ain't so sure that's a good thing."

He sits alone, primarily in silence, as the soldiers do their thing. He's not a soldier, he's actually a member of the organization, handpicked by Jonathan Harlow for this job. The first convoy is gone, carrying the remnants of whatever emerged from the mine and didn't die in a hail of gunfire. Three or four only, including Jack Harlow's companion – but not his friend, not the hunter. Mostly, Lance doesn't care what happened in the mine. He's only concerned about one of them.

He knows he's being watched. He knows Brina's got more eyes than her own. He knows the residents of Silver Blade, hidden away as they are now, would rip off his head given the chance. The survivors of the shallow city in the mine – they would do it slowly.

The stories are inconsistent and untrustworthy. An uprising? A battle spanning four levels of the shallow city. The arrival of the DarkWalker upset and ended everything. The prison is gone. Devastated and demolished. The Council will not be pleased. They will be disappointed with the performance of Lance Turner, and they will not be happy with Jonathon Harlow. As far as the Council is concerned, Jack Harlow is disposable.

Outside, the dawn is stark and brings no warmth. The sun's light casts long shadows through the mountains. The silence is overwhelming.

Lance Turner may be many things, but he's no seer. However, the silence isn't merely an omen to read. It's a sign, an indication, that something's coming, something's risen from the mine, and today the soldiers will earn their pay.

He didn't even taste his drink. He waves for another. Brina growls as she responds. She'll be well paid, too. It's only money, and it's not his.

CHAPTER TWO

JOHN URBANCIK

1.

Jack Harlow walks into Silver Blade.

He walks alone, hands outstretched like a messiah, like a deliverer of good news. Soldiers follow him. Soldiers flank him. Soldiers in front of him back away as he advances. No less than a dozen weapons aim at his head and chest, but he is not afraid. He's never been good with fear. It's not something he understands. The thing he most feared in all his life happened when Lisa Sparrow sacrificed herself to save him.

He walks slowly, deliberately, aware of every quickened heartbeat. He can read these men, these soldiers, these mercenaries who are about to give their lives for money. Jack Harlow is not a watcher and never has been. He's a DarkWalker.

He spent days or years or lifetimes under the earth, in the presence of vampires, ogres, shadows, revenants, and darkness. He doesn't know the full extent of what he's absorbed, and he's never understood it before. He's never been so strong, so dangerous, so volatile. It's an effort to restrain himself. His palms are up, a sign of surrender. In the center of town, not far from the Fox and Silver Sparrow, Jack Harlow stops and examines his circumstances and chooses one of the soldiers ahead of him. "Run," he says, and he can't help that it sounds like a threat, "and fetch your master."

The soldier responds by speaking into a device on his shoulder. "The package has entered the town. I repeat, the package has walked unarmed into Silver Blade."

The response is swift: "Do not engage." Even tinny and electronicized, Lance Turner's voice is recognizable. His inflections are unique, a foundation of Liverpool British and a scattering of corruptions from across the world.

"Too late," Jack Harlow says, too softly for anyone to hear. He grins. It feels good, this degree of wickedness and anticipation.

In their uniforms, in their goggles and their armor, the soldiers are no more human than the dogs that served in the mine. He looks from one to another, not bothering to turn to see the pair behind him and not acknowledging the four who think they're hiding in the rooftops. Just these six he can see. He sees into them in ways he's never known possible. He can see the blood move in their veins with every beat of their hearts. He clearly sees the object of their attention – himself, reflected in their gazes – at least they've hired men with focus. Not a one glances into the forest behind him. Not one looks to the sky.

On the rooftops, Sibyl, a Sister of Shadow, slips between two of the hidden soldiers. She touches one at the small of his back through his gear and through his armor and through his flesh, touches the very heart of him. The organ withers and decays. The other feels her hand on the back of his neck. The electricity overloads his nervous system, paralyzing every muscle. He never has a chance to cry out as tendrils of pain ignite. Inside, he screams, and it's an awful thing to hear, but he dies in silence.

On another rooftop, Colton works a spell that robs the soldiers of their minds. First their memories, then their motor functions, and finally their involuntary processes.

On the ground, only Jack Harlow is aware of this. The eight soldiers surrounding him are extraordinary in their intensity and their stupidity.

Lance Turner comes down the street. He looks like a proper British gentleman, maybe short a cane or umbrella. He holds himself well, despite the alcohol. He's been drinking. Why would that be? Jack Harlow looks deeper, peels away layers of his "handler", spying on his very soul. Ambitious, but defeated and lost.

"You can't tell me any more lies," Jack Harlow tells him.

"I've never lied to you."

"You know you have."

The two soldiers ahead of Jack part to let Lance step forward, but he takes only one step past them. "You're surrounded."

"So it would appear," Jack admits.

"They changed my orders after you went in."

"*That*," Jack tells him, "does not ring true."

"The mine was a trap," Lance admits.

"They thought they had the perfect bait."

Lance shakes his head. "The perfect bait is beyond us. But they thought they could use your vampire hunter friend. They did consider other options."

"I escaped."

"You destroyed it. That was..." Lance doesn't find the right word to finish it.

"It doesn't matter anymore," Jack Harlow says. "You're bringing me in."

"What?"

"I'll go willingly." He holds up his hands as if they're cuffed together. "I won't resist."

"I'd rather not."

Jack Harlow smiles. "I'm afraid you don't have a choice."

Lance Turner smiles, but the smile is a lie. "They'll kill you where you stand."

"Is that what you want?"

It's not. Even the soldiers know that.

Jack stands so that the sun is behind him. It's low but rising. The shadows across the nearly abandoned city of Silver Blade are long and deep, but the creatures moving among them are unconcerned with sunlight. A great many things exist in the dark, but not all are subjugated to it.

Gunfire cuts the morning.

"You didn't kill everything that got out of the mine."

"When we knew it would fall, we had no choice."

Jack Harlow ignores it. "Where's Naomi?"

"Not here."

Jack Harlow takes one step. The effect is everything he intended: the soldiers raise their already raised weapons. Lance Turner retreats a step. Something howls in the east. Someone screams in the west. Someone fires a high-capacity automatic weapon. Before these eight soldiers can react, before they can do more than think about the triggers, they're surrounded. Beaumont Laurent, the gnome, appears first. Then a ghost. A vampire. Sibyl, the Sister of Shadow. Rana leaps forward to sit at Jack's side. He lowers a hand to scratch behind the beast's ears.

One of the soldiers gets off a shot. Eulalia, with a thin curved blade Jack never saw underground, slices his throat.

The bullet vanishes, its business undone.

Jack Harlow steps toward Lance again, and this time there's nowhere to go; Sibyl is behind him like a glacier. He says, as the eight soldiers around them drop, "Take me to her."

2.

Preparations are simple. There's a truck with eight cells ready to move to another facility. It sounds like there's an endless supply of such places, but the organization is stretched. Although they're tasked with watching and recording and maintaining, whatever that means, lately there's been more activity. Something's happened.

It's very vague, reading people, and tiring. Jack Harlow gets little from Lance he didn't already know. All his soldiers are dead. The city has been returned to its own ashes. Brina stands outside the Fox and Silver Sparrow absentmindedly wiping a silver stein as she watches an unnatural darkness fall over the city.

City was never the right word for this place. It's a collection of a dozen unstable structures a hundred and fifty years old over an abandoned mine that, until recently, served as a prison pit for darkness. The watchers never really knew what went on down there. They basically sealed the mine, arranged for little or nothing to be able to get out, and left it alone until *someone* decided to make use of it again. The denizens of Silver Blade had been about to rise, regardless, so maybe the timing had been fortuitous.

Someone had decided to condemn Jack Harlow, DarkWalker, to the pit.

Someone named Jonathan Harlow. Jack's father.

"They know what happened," Lance tells Jack. The back of the truck is filled with former residents of the shallow city. The locks are false.

Lance likes to refer to the organization as *they*, but he really means Jonathon Harlow, as though Jack's father was the head of this beast. Jack can count off a list of the wrongs done to him by his father over the years. In retrospect. And his sister, Lizzie. The secrets. The lies. Jack turns inward, locating the tracking device – and its drop of poison – hidden inside him. It shines under his skin. He draws in a lungful of air, all the way down to his balls, and disables it. With an audible crack, its signal dies, its poison goes inert, and it disintegrates.

Lance is about to put the truck in gear. It's a big rig, as big as could reach the city, larger and more difficult than the Land Rover. Those keys are in his room at the Fox and Silver Sparrow. If Lance doesn't return, Brina will likely use it to leave this wasteland.

Jack Harlow has no feelings for Brina, one way or another. He has no feelings for Lance except a mild distaste. The man's only done what he thought was right, even if he wasn't.

Lance tries one last time. "You don't have to do this."

"I'm giving you a chance to redeem yourself."

"Do you think you can just walk in and destroy the whole organization?"

"There's only one, maybe two, I'm currently concerned with."

Lance Turner shakes his head as he starts the truck rolling. "And what if they don't let you walk away?"

"I'll forgive them," Jack Harlow says. It sounds worse than he means it, but it doesn't matter because it's a lie. "The watchers have been interfering. Not playing by the rules."

"Whose rules?"

Jack Harlow stares straight ahead at the dirt road. He doesn't know how to answer this, but he wants to tell the truth. Some things feel important. "Do you know there's always been a DarkWalker?" Jack doesn't leave enough time for an answer. "Since before history, since before humanity, since before a conglomeration of rocks and dust formed the earth, there has been a DarkWalker. I am not alone."

"The files don't contain anything other than you."

"That's because the watchers have been doing a horrible job."

"Then what is it?" Lance asked. "What's a DarkWalker, if not a glorified watcher?"

Jack Harlow laughs – with almost true humor – but he doesn't answer.

3.

Naomi feels the sun rise. There are no windows in this prison, which is more modern and harsher than the prison under Silver Blade. She's alone in a cell six feet by six, which wouldn't be sufficient to contain some of the creatures she'd seen in the truck when they brought her here. The bed is a metal plank, presumably laced with silver and lead and whatever other metals they think will subdue their charges. The walls are solid something, probably thick, and probably thicker when necessary.

She'd set the mine of Silver Blade ablaze, but it had cost her all her strength. She barely escaped, and ran straight into Lance Turner. Of the organization. She wants to get her fingers around his throat. She's not often prone to violent tendencies. She wants to rip through his ribs and feed on his organs, a thing which she absolutely does not require.

They took her pouch. Her bag of goodies. They judged her and stuck her with needles to draw blood and they kept her sedated, not quite unconscious, until they finally got her into her own cell.

She's still weak. They don't trust her to swallow medicine, so it's injections four times a day. They don't allow her to maintain any sort of sleep schedule. Armed guards patrol outside, checking on her through the little eye slit in the door, and a camera in the corner of the ceiling watches her every move. They offer no privacy, just a flat surface for sleeping and a toilet and a sink. Not even a book to read. If she could at least pass her time with a good book, she might not have to build up such a level of resentment for her captors.

These are, somehow, in a convoluted way, Jack Harlow's people, but they are against him. She doesn't pretend to understand. She doesn't even pretend to care. She recites words, good words, old words, under her breath so that if they've got microphones in her cell they'll only hear her breathing. She moves her fingers, for all the world a person merely flexing sore fists. Elsewhere in this prison, others exercise their fists by pounding out a thunderous rhythm on the thick, solid doors. She imagines bloodied fists but a level of persistence that can only be admired. The rhythm is good. Comforting. It fits with what she's doing, so she steals it and uses it. When the guard looks in through the eye slit, she looks back and smiles coyly and averts her gaze. He slides a plastic tray of food through the opening in the floor. It's a bowl of mush, a cup of water. They don't intend to starve her to death. That's something.

She listens as best she can. Her hearing is not supernatural, but she applies a bit of magic to the task and explores the sounds. Men pissing in the restrooms. Guards joking in a room full of monitors with full sound from every cell. The whimpering of something merely a dog, an honest dog rather than the wretched things living in the mines. She cannot make out words, but over the course of days she begins to recognize the rhythms.

The mush that passes as food passes right through her. They might not be poisoning her, but the combination of that crap and the drugs do terrible things to her digestive system. As if she needed a reason to get out of this place.

Medicine, food, eyes checking through the door. Medicine, food, eyes. She's got track marks on her arm like a junkie, but through her scars they're unnoticeable to anyone else. They're not skilled. The drugs are not administered by trained nurses, but by brute strength and domination.

She does what she can to counteract the medicine. It's a strong sedative. It dulls pain, dulls her senses, and it's difficult to neutralize. But she manages, through willpower and mystical incantations, to minimize it. As she regains strength, she doesn't show it. Eventually, after almost a week, she manages to isolate the medicine in her veins, direct it through her kidneys, and eliminate it at the toilet in full view of the watchers and their camera lenses. She doesn't look up to smile at them, though she's tempted.

Naomi pays attention to the rhythms, and when the time is right, when they come in for her next dosage, she slips sideways through time and past her guards.

The alarm is raised immediately. She's got two, maybe three slips available to her before the collapses, so she mostly runs through the long, dark corridors. She has no lay of the land, no real idea how to escape, but she follows the sounds that have, over the past week or so, been most promising. Through one corridor and another, through stairs, finally to a loading dock, where a team of armed guards want to open fire. She slips past them, and finally outside, and settles into a hole not far from the facility, not far from the river, not far from anything at all.

4.

The ride is a miasma of awkward silence. Jack Harlow barely even notices Lance, and doesn't respond to questions or comments. He stares out the window thinking about friends and family and lovers and monsters. He's never known anything else.

He tries not to think of his father or sister, and instead wonders about his mother, her role in all this. She must've been part of the organization as well. Her car, the Mustang she'd given him a long time ago, sits in a driveway in Westchester.

"I'll need to refuel," Lance tells him. Jack barely nods in acknowledgement. His thoughts drift to the house on Long Island where he first saw a ghost, a ghost no longer there and a house no longer there. He shifts to an apartment in Orlando where the love of his life died.

Lisa Sparrow. They'd met at a place called *The Precipice*, which in retrospect seemed appropriate. He hadn't believed in love, thought *love at first sight* was a fancy way of describing *lust*. But that first moment, everything Jack knew changed. He'd been running his whole life, trying to evade the darkness yet embracing it every stop along the road, until she told him – what did she tell him, exactly? She made promises with her heart, body, and soul, and he wished very much they'd been able to see those promises fulfilled.

But he'd lived in ignorance, of what he was and what really existed in the darkness. He'd been half convinced it was all in his head, a psychotic breakdown of some sort, hallucinations he couldn't control.

Now the visions are completely out of control.

He feels the restlessness from the back of the truck. His new friends. He's never been good at friends, and had been lured to Silver Blade – lured by Lance Turner, out there now putting gas into this truck – because of a debt. Nick Hunter had stood by him the night Lisa died. The vampire Jia Li had also been there. The effort meant something, means something even now.

One day, he'll go back. When all this is done, when his friends are safe, when the organization is no more, when his father has paid for his crimes.

Lance Turner climbs back into the truck and offers a bottle of water. Jack Harlow stares. "It's not poison," Lance tells him.

Jack Harlow takes the water. "If you're still alive when this is done," he says, "what will you do?"

Lance stares back at him. His eyes are shallow. They weren't always. "I'll persevere."

"And me?" Jack Harlow asks.

"What makes you think you'll survive whatever this is?"

Jack Harlow smiles. It's genuine. He barely remembers what that feels like. He says, "Drive."

In Pennsylvania, they abandon the interstates. The roads twist and rise and drop, and they pass perilously close to structures built right at the edge of the road. There are bare cornfields and lots of forest, and even after leaving the interstate it's hours before they get close to their destination. It's not quite dusk, but the sun is low when Jack Harlow first sees the Susquehanna River.

It's a mystery to Jack Harlow. He grew up on Long Island, so the only thing he knows about this part of the world is Three Mile Island. And now the watchers, organized for some obscure purpose, have a facility somewhere along this shore. It's wide, as far as rivers go, but Jack's used to staring across the Long Island Sound trying to make out the edge of Connecticut on the horizon. On the opposite shore, some houses have turned on their lights. Lit buoys float in the water. A boat paces them headed upriver. A shade of pink is settling over the sky.

"It's another few miles," Lance Turner says. "They're not expecting me, you know."

"But they are expecting a truck."

When they arrive, the facility is as understated as possible, merely a warehouse on the edge of the river, with a dock and a parking lot and a network of underground tunnels. Jack Harlow can feel the hollowness beneath them as they pull up to guard shack. It's just one man in some generic uniform with a cap and a mustache. Lance rolls down the window and hands the guard his identification.

The guard glances at Jack Harlow in the passenger seat.

Jack gets a quick assessment of the man: single and lonely, troubled and anxious, a bit heavy on the violent side but likes to think he's got it under control. A drinking problem, not just beer anymore, and the occasional line of cocaine for kicks. He's seen things he can't explain and doesn't want to be here and is afraid something will break out of the underground cells, something big but unspecified, something he imagines exists but might not. And now, with Jack Harlow staring back at him, the guard is realizing all his fears do exist. Jack offers a smile, but it's not friendly and it's not warm. The guard scans Lance's ID with an electronic device, says, "Wait here," and retreats into the safety of his shack.

It's a new way of seeing for Jack.

The guard speaks into an old phone with a tangled cord. The words don't penetrate the glass, but the guard shoots two distinct glances in Jack's direction during the conversation. His answers are short, the call quick, and he sticks his head out of the shack long enough to say, "Go on in, Mr. Turner." He's got a hand on his holstered sidearm, and he's waiting for an excuse to pull it.

Inside, the warehouse is a wide space with three other trucks, a dozen Jeeps and Land Rovers, and one gleaming, sharp-edged Lincoln Town Car from the 80's. Someone's taken care of it, someone other than Jack Harlow's father. He didn't really expect to run into his dad here. That would've been too easy.

Lance pulls the truck to the side, then backs it toward a loading dock. The beeping agitates everyone in the truck. Some had slept, or at least rested, during the drive, but everyone and everything back there is alert now. Jack can feel their growing anticipation through the wall of the truck as if it's a solid thing. The truck bumps against the dock, and men, the organization's men, are already moving before Jack Harlow can climb out.

5.

According to Lance Turner, twenty armed guards patrol these corridors. Their armament varies, and is designed to handle the types of things they hold. There are, including a previous shipment of creatures from Silver Blade, no less than a dozen creatures in cells. A half dozen watchers work out of the Susquehanna facility, and there's any number of other operatives, administrative personnel and the like.

Jack Harlow walks alongside the truck, toward the back, where the workers are already rolling open a new kind of hell. Rana's first out of the back of the truck. She's not used to being cooped up for any amount of time, so the first man at the door is the first man whose ribs shatter when she attacks. Even in armor, he's unprepared, but they're soldiers and they're supposed to be ready for anything and there's no telling what they've seen.

Colton, the warlock, unleashes a spell he's presumably been planning for most of the past eight hours. The explosion of darkness blinds the soldiers, at least momentarily.

They almost work like an actual team.

One of the soldiers yanks Eulalia from the back of the truck. Another shoots Sibyl, one of the Sisters of Shadow, but this facility isn't designed to hold specters or phantasms or anything else insubstantial.

Not that they won't be prepared for it.

But they were expecting vampires, ogres, ghouls, and other physical manifestations of darkness and evil. They weren't expecting an organized response. They weren't expecting resistance of any sort. The creatures were meant to be sedated and in cages.

Beaumont emerges from the truck and crushes heads in his hands. He smiles, and says, "Fuck, yeah!"

Jack Harlow is not enjoying himself. He hops onto the loading platform and taps the shoulder of the soldier holding Eulalia. The guy turns, but he's already dead, and the girl – he'd thought of her as a girl, but now he realizes he'd been wrong – is smiling and holding a long, thin blade.

The soldiers are not without resources. One blasts the head off a vampire. Another's shot gets the warlock in the shoulder. As Colton spins and drops, Beaumont smashes through the soldier's chest. When Sibyl laughs, only Jack Harlow can hear her, and it's chilling.

Lance Turner climbs onto the platform. Four dead soldiers and two dock men lay in pieces and in pools of blood. One is moaning but not really still alive. Another twitches. Rana's still digging through one of the bodies, tearing out chunks of meat and swallowing them whole. The lights have gone red.

"That," Lance Turner says, "was your element of surprise."

"It was fucking satisfying," Beaumont says.

Eulalia kneels next to Colton, whose eyes are closed. "I think he's going to die."

"All of you will, one day," Jack tells her.

It's not the answer she wants, but she stands anyhow. All the doors have been locked down. There's no place to go except through them. They're likely thick and problematic. Jack asks Lance, "Can they hear us?"

"Probably."

Jack Harlow looks up at the nearest camera. He holds out his hands, palms up again, claiming he's unarmed and not a threat despite this brief display. "You know who I am," he tells the camera, "and you know what I want. So I'll give you a choice." He considers the possibilities. "You can live to see another dawn. Or die horribly."

Beaumont cracks his knuckles. They sound like bricks.

Colton coughs and opens his eyes briefly. He's working on himself, applying all his magical healing to his wound. The bullet went through him, left holes on both sides, but they're close together and missed the major organs. There's a lot of blood, but he's got plenty more and he knows when he'll die. Jack takes Eulalia's hand and squeezes it. "He's not going to die. Not yet."

A door opens. It's a narrow door, sturdy but small, far enough to the side that no one can reach it quickly. No one moves. A watcher emerges, surrounded by his natural aura of protection. He walks toward the group of them, all creatures of darkness except maybe Lance Turner. He has a haunted look Jack recognizes.

"Sister of Shadow, gnome, warlock, frog," the watcher says. "Two humans, one scarred and one a traitor, and the DarkWalker."

"*A* DarkWalker."

The watcher's eyes go up at that. "So there's more than one of you?"

"You're not stupid enough to think I'll believe you didn't know."

"What I know," the watcher says, "doesn't matter."

"You think you're safe."

"Not from her." He glances at Eulalia.

"Are you here to negotiate?" Jack asks. "I thought I made my terms clear."

"You have." The watcher smiles. He's young, maybe college age, and he's confident he can walk untouched through hell. He doesn't know that Jack's done it, and that immunity isn't as strong as it seems.

Beaumont, for a moment seeming ready to put his fists to the task, deflates and says, "Fuck."

Jack Harlow knows that immunity. It's like a shield. It attracts and repels, and can be inverted. He says, "Do you know imps?"

"You were changed by one."

"I was always a DarkWalker," Jack Harlow says. "Your files need updating. I was changed, yes, but not into what I am."

"You attracted the dark. It descended on you. I know."

"Then you know," Jack Harlow says. He pauses and takes a breath. He believes what he's about to say, but he's not entirely sure. It's untested. "You know I can make you vulnerable."

The watcher meets Jack's eyes but says nothing. It's not a steady gaze. There's fear in there somewhere, deep and hidden and neglected, but this watcher isn't dumb. "We don't know anything," he says. "The DarkWalker is something of a mystery to us." He glances at Lance Turner, then back to Jack. "The file is empty."

That, Jack Harlow doesn't expect. And he doesn't believe it. Not that this watcher is lying to him; Jack think he'd know. "All you do is create files."

"Not *all* we do," the watcher says, taking in the entire warehouse with a quick gesture of his hand.

"Are you the only watcher here?"

"We're rarer than you may think."

"I thought there might be six."

"We tend to work in the field."

"Then why are you here?"

The watcher takes a breath and glances at Lance. "I was called in for..." He doesn't know what word to use, and when he finds it he doesn't want to use it. "Processing."

"Who called you in?"

Another glance at Lance. The handler. This time, Jack looks, too. "Is this your facility?"

"I worked out of here, yes."

"Are you in charge?"

"No."

"Were you?"

Lance hesitates. "No."

"Just fucking kill him," Beaumont says. "He ain't giving up your girl."

"I can't do that," the watcher says. Jack must wear his reaction on the outside, because the watcher takes half a step back and adds quickly, "She's not here."

"Transferred?" Lance asks.

"Escaped."

A long moment of silence follows that. The watcher is telling the truth. Jack can see it in his eyes and hear it in his voice. He sees it in the way the watcher's blood flows through his veins. Jack's not used to this kind of vision, but he trusts it. He trusts himself. He understands the changes overtaking him. Finally, Jack Harlow shakes and lowers his head. "That's too bad."

And his army – is that what they are? – the Sister of Shadow, the gnome, and Rana – turn their attentions to the big, thick, heavy door before them, through which the cells would have been transported.

Eulalia kneels beside Colton, who's sitting up now. He adds some spell work to the effort. It doesn't take long. First, there's a single crack in the steel alloys of the door. It expands, stretches high and low, then splinters like a spider's web. The watcher steps back to watch, which is all he's good for. Lance steps away as well. He has nothing to contribute here.

The cracks start to come away in bits, then in hunks, until finally a hole opens up. Bullets start flying through the hole. They pass through Sibyl. They leave scratches on Beaumont's face. Three seconds of this, and the hole is large enough to go through.

Sibyl didn't need the hole, but she seems happy to contribute to the cause. She gives Jack a look – it's hard to interpret, because she's all shadow and no feature – but appears happy. Thrilled, even. For all of them, this is a moment of vengeance.

Sibyl slips through the hole and shatters the souls of soldiers. Beaumont crashes through it and shatters bones and faces and bodies. Rana leaps through and buries her teeth in fresh flesh, something she was denied – they were all denied – in the pits of Silver Blade.

The smoke might be anyone's fault, their side or the enemy's. It doesn't stop the rampage.

"You shouldn't have done this," the watcher says.

"You shouldn't have done any of this," Jack Harlow tells him.

Eulalia moves to help Colton to his feet, but Jack puts out a hand. "Rest. I don't need you to die for me."

Colton smiles weakly. "I don't intend to, but fate is unwavering."

Is his wound that serious? Jack kneels beside him, examines the bullet hole which has already started to mend, the blood which has stopped flowing. "Poison?"

"Laced with something," Colton says.

Jack looks to the watcher. "With what?"

"Arsenic, strychnine, silver, garlic, wolfsbane, cyanide, belladonna, nightshade." The watcher pauses. "I'm probably leaving something out, but any or all of that."

Jack shakes his head. "Not taking any chances."

"It's something synthetic," Colton says. "I don't recognize the sensation of it."

"You've been underground a long time," Jack tells him.

"I'll be underground again soon." Colton grimaces. "But I've developed immunities to most flora."

"Is there an antidote?" Eulalia asks the watcher.

"Unlikely."

The warlock's veins run bright red under his skin and rise to the surface. They're hot to the touch. Jack turns to Eulalia. "Give me your knife."

"My knife?"

"Quickly."

She hands it over. The blade is long and narrow and solid. She says, "It's tainted, you know."

"With nothing Colton cannot resist," Jack says. He slices open one of the veins in Colton's forearm. The warlock flinches. Blood spills. Jack reaches under the skin and into the vein, into the flow of blood. He diverts it, pulling the toxins out along his finger, up his wrist and forearm, to his elbow before they stream down to the ground. He leaves the blood inside, pulling only what's bad, but it's not major enough an artery. He leans close and says, "I'm going to need something stronger, something closer to the heart."

"And brain," Colton says. "I think I'm hearing voices."

"So am I, actually," the watcher says.

So is Jack, but he's ignoring them. Keeping a hand on the vein, which he cannot actually reseal, he opens Colton's carotid artery in his neck.

The blood pulses and spits, but it's weakened. Jack reaches in, using both hands now – Eulalia puts pressure on Colton's arm – and conducts the toxins away from the brain, draws them from the warlock's body and dispels them in a way he didn't even know he could do.

The watcher makes a sound of disbelief or surprise, but he's beyond Jack's caring.

Lance kneels on the other side of Colton to help keep him propped in a seated position. The extra blood loss might kill him before the poison has a chance to work.

"There's damage," Jack says, seeing discoloration in the lungs and heart and liver and kidneys, seeing this despite the skin, through the blood somehow. "Old damage, new damage, it's beyond me. You're going to die, Colton, and you're going to die soon."

Colton manages to focus his gray eyes on Jack's. "I wanted my vengeance, too."

Jack says, "You'll have it."

6.

Vengeance, a distant relation to Justice, can be an ugly thing. Jack Harlow's army, his own personal soldiers, go through the facility with extreme prejudice.

Rana races down the halls, enjoying the symmetry and levelness, loving the twists and turns, reveling in the fresh meat. She follows the scents, chases the sounds, and gorges herself as she hasn't since the days of her good doctor, her first master, when the world was plainer and less scary.

Beau Laurent crushes things and shatters things. He makes no differentiation between bones and machinery. Within minutes, he's drenched with blood, but the soldiers do some real damage to him. He was never going to live forever. He's old. He's been away from his home for far too long. The mine, and the caves under that mine, were a poor substitute for his mountain across the great pond. Maybe when he dies, he'll return – if only in his dreams. He rounds a corner, and there's a soldier with some variation of heavy artillery, something designed to cause damage, to blast things apart. It's some sort of missile, inappropriate for the space, but a good soldier's got to be prepared for whatever comes along. Beau takes a breath and, under his breath, says "Fuck" one last time before the soldiers launches the shattering weapon.

Sibyl touches soldiers and liquefies their flesh. She touches a button that opens the cells, all the cages, releasing everything they've been holding and hiding here by the river. She's satisfied, at least as far as her thirsts go, and she's repaid the DarkWalker for his act of kindness which released her from the prison. She draws a breath – it's almost air she needs – and goes in search of her sisters. Once upon a time, they were three, and they will be three again. The DarkWalker doesn't need her.

The creatures, beasts, and people released from the prison, even in their drug-addled states, even weakened and tortured, even those who have been subjected to experimentation, overwhelm the remaining soldiers. Before it's over, the entire underground facility plunges into complete, utter darkness, so that even the smoke and unnatural mists cannot be seen. Not everything survives. One or two don't even leave their cells. They've already wasted away.

Above, outside the warehouse, one guard remains in the shack outside, the door closed tight as if it will protect him. He listens to cries for help and cries of agony over the radio. He shudders when the earth trembles and sends ripples up and down the Susquehanna River. They probably feel it as far away as Lehorn's Hollow. He watches as the inmates run free into the night. Nightmares, these things are. He turns out his light and hopes to hide in the dark. Something, however, won't let him. It lands on the ceiling. He draws his gun. He's got armor piercing bullets laced with silver and weaponized venom of some sort. His finger's steady even if his heart's breaking speed records. He crouches, he focuses his attention on the sounds, the movement and shuffling above, the snuffling. It's a beast of some sort, not something he can reason with. One of the wolves or a variation thereof. Or that damned over-sized spider thing. He doesn't want to know. He wants it to just go away. He holds his breath a moment to listen better. There's something crawling outside, too. And there's something that shouldn't be on the river. Something that shouldn't be on the road. Is he hallucinating now? These weren't things they held here. He grabs the phone, dials an outside number, waits only one ring before it's picked up on the other side, but only silence answers. He says, "The Susquehanna facility is compromised." After a brief moment, there's a click on the other side and the line goes dead. Then the window crashes in on him, shards of glass and claws. He gets a shot off, another and another, but then the thing in the darkness is shredding his flesh and scraping his bones. He's proud of himself. He doesn't cry out. He doesn't succumb to panic or terror. He merely dies.

JOHN URBANCIK

CHAPTER THREE

1.

As Eulalia helps the warlock clean up, as Rana comes bounding back up the stairs, Jack Harlow looks at, and into, the watcher, and shakes his head. "I don't know what to do with you."

The watcher doesn't answer. He stands straight. He controls his trembling. He's questioning his immunity to the darkness. Everything around him has been destroyed, and it happened so fast he could do nothing to stop it. No one else from this facility still lives except the prisoners, who have all been released to either run free or die at their choice. Lance Turner's outside looking out over the river. The two had probably known each other. Worked with each other.

"What do you suggest?" Jack asks.

"Kill me," the watcher says. "If you can."

"You're an idiot, you know that? I could shoot you, without ever touching you, and not risk that burning repulsion that keeps most creatures at bay. The aura surrounding you, the one that means most the night doesn't even bother to look at you, it's part of me. I have your experience. You can't engage with it like you have here without interfering with your own protections." He doesn't seem to be making an impact, so he steps closer, close enough to whisper, close enough to maul the watcher's throat if he wished. "You are not immune."

"We all die," the watcher says.

"Eventually. Why are you in such a hurry?"

The watcher grins. Jack admires it. He didn't know how it felt to be on the receiving end of one of those. "If you wanted to kill me, I'd already be dead."

"There is that."

"Unless you want information."

Jack nods toward Lance at the edge of the river. "I've got that."

"Did you turn him? Do you control him?"

Jack gives Lance a longer look. He'd coerced him, sure, but that doesn't account for everything the handler has done tonight. He could've resisted. He could have fled. He might have taken a cyanide pill to avoid exactly what's happening now. The man, with his proper British accent and proper manners and bookish attributes, looks back at Jack without a smile. "He was assigned to be my handler," Jack says. "He even brought me in. The only traitor here is me."

"You were a rogue," the watcher says.

"Is that what they say?"

"Rogue," the watcher says, "or Ronin, whatever you prefer. Out there on your own, serving no master, following no rules, obeying no laws."

Jack Harlow laughs. It's a good, honest laugh, the first he's had in too long. He takes a breath and flexes the sore muscles in his back. It's full dark outside now, the sun sunken and the pink of sunset vanished. "I see further than I used to," Jack tells the watcher. "You named us when you came into the warehouse, but I can look out at that city, that town, and from here I can pick out a magus and a nest of vipers and a dozen ghosts or more, an ogre and a lost soul and even a wandering reverend. My sight, my vision, has improved."

"Because you're not a watcher."

"Not merely a watcher. I never was. It was just that – I was always close to them. My father. My sister."

"Your mother," the watcher says.

"You think you know everything."

"I know enough."

"You think you have something to trade?"

"I must," the watcher says. "Or like you say, you could just shoot me."

The beast, Rana, comes bounding out of the depths of the warehouse. Her body is slick with blood, her eyes wild, her froglike smile unmistakable even on her inhuman face. She comes up to Jack Harlow's side and nuzzles against his leg. He scratches the back of her head and says, "You don't need a master anymore, Rana. You're free."

She looks up at him and, for a moment, he's not sure she understands. "Go, be wild, be yourself," he tells Rana. "Be your own master. You owe me nothing, you owe your service to no one, not even your good doctor."

She rolls her head to press against his hand, then makes a froglike sound that somehow says she doesn't think of him as a master but as a friend.

Jack motions to the forest across the street. "Anywhere and anything you want, Rana."

She yips, something almost doglike, almost catlike, and lopes to the edge of the river. She sniffs at Lance briefly, looks back at Jack and says, in a broken, cracked, unnatural voice that barely manages to form the words, "Thank you." Then she jumps into the Susquehanna River.

No one else rises from the warehouse. The gnome and the Sister of Shadow are dead or gone. Which is fine by Jack. He didn't know the extent of his own strength.

"You're alone now," the watcher says.

"I've always been alone."

"Except that night with..." The watcher hesitates, searching his memory to make sure he gets the name right, and it's the worst possible thing he can say. "Lisa Sparrow. The DarkWalker's lover, dead and gone."

The echo of his own thoughts adds to Jack's fury. He grabs the watcher by the throat. He feels the watcher's power, that gentle repulsion, that heated resistance, at a cellular level, but it's insignificant. Jack Harlow functioned as a watcher for far too long to be turned away by it.

He lifts the watcher off his feet, crushing his windpipe with a blood-soaked hand. He'd briefly thought he'd let the watcher go, let him risk the wrath of creatures he'd once held that were now free in the night. Now, blood seeps from the watcher's nose, ears, and eyes. And while it's Jack doing the damage, it's not just his *hand*.

The watcher struggles. He grabs at Jack's hand, he claws at the skin, he thrashes in search of a breath. By squeezing just a little more tightly, Jack crushes the watcher's windpipe and vertebrae and spirit.

He lets the corpse drop.

"That," Lance Turner says from the edge of the river, fifty feet away, "was unkind."

Jack Harlow closes his eyes and looks inward. He's still him, somewhere inside of him, he's still in control and entirely himself, but he's so much more now.

"The mine changed you," Lance says.

Jack knows it's true. He strides across the parking lot. The warehouse behind him looks as it always had, plus three or four tendrils of smoke that are virtually invisible under the night clouds. "The Deep City changed me," Jack says. "What was beneath the Deep City."

At the surface, the mining town of Silver Blade stood above the Shallow City of Silver Blade, which had been a prison of sorts for the things of the dark, a multi-leveled hell on earth designed to keep those creatures tamed, at each other's throats, and contained. Beneath that, there had been the Deep City, and the kinds of secrets the organization did not understand.

"Yes and no," Jack says. "I was a DarkWalker, and I am a DarkWalker. But I know what that means now."

"What does it mean?"

"Strength," Jack says. "Incomprehensible power. I don't believe for a minute there's no file."

"I've never seen a DarkWalker file. Just yours."

"My father's seen it," Jack says. "Where is he?"

"I can't possibly know that."

"You saw what I did to your friend," Jack says. "To your facility. You can walk away now, but point me in the right direction." He lowers his voice to add a threat. "Point me in the wrong direction, and there's no place on earth you'll be able to hide."

Lance Turner's pulse betray him. The handler believes him. "Jonathan Harlow travels," he says, his voice hitched half an octave higher than normal. "He's one of the Council."

"Council?"

"You know nothing, do you?"

"Tell me now."

"The Council runs the order. They're the overseers."

"The order?"

"The Order of the White Raven," Lance says. "It's an old name, but it's the official name."

"And the splinter group?"

"I don't know what you mean."

Jack believes him. "Okay, then, tell me this. Where is Elizabeth?" His sister.

Lance Turner hesitates. He doesn't want to answer. He doesn't have a choice. "She's probably in New York."

"Where?"

Lance gives him an address in Manhattan. Calls it The Brownstone. "Or she's in the field. She's an operative."

"And tell me this," Jack Harlow says. "What is it the Ravens are really watching for?"

But Lance Turner obviously has no idea what he means.

2.

The river is never still. There's always boats and fish and wind and whatever else makes the waves, and there's Naomi sleeping and healing in a cocoon of her own making. It blends into the night and the day, it hides within plain sight, it escapes any form of detection, and it wakes her after the sun has fallen.

She's on the other side of the river from the facility, not far from the bridge that is U.S. 30. She's sweat all traces of the sedatives out of her system. Her mind is alert and clear. Physically, she's not at one hundred percent, but she's close.

The facility, she sees, isn't at one hundred percent anymore, either. She doesn't want to bring attention to herself. She doesn't have her pouch anymore; it's back in Silver Blade somewhere, possibly lost forever. So she has to make do with what she's got. She pulls gently from the water, from the fish and algae and bacteria, from the microscopic life floating on its surface. She pulls from the nearby spiders and the mayflies and, as much as she can, from the stars themselves.

Ultimately, it's a raven that gives her vision.

What she sees frightens her: Jack Harlow, the DarkWalker, standing on the edge of the river like a god, Lance Turner beside him and still alive, the facility smoldering behind them. She cannot count the days since she was brought here, but she knows she's less than a day from her escape. They probably suspect she's further away than she is.

She sees something she's never seen before: power pulsating from the DarkWalker and raw anger. His time under the mine has changed him, yes, but it's awakened him to what he is. Maybe this is, maybe this isn't, a good thing.

She desperately wants to see Lance Turner bleed to death. She wants to stand over him with his heart in her hand and a smile on her face. But that's not going to happen. His fate, whatever it will be, is out of her hands. And so is the DarkWalker's.

He came looking for her. By now, he must know she's not there. He's destroyed the facility and released everything within.

She's got to be smart. He can see now, see in ways he might not fully understand yet. Her protective cocoon is weak and temporary. She needs a better disguise, so she fashions a glamour, nothing spectacular, something like a cloak. She doesn't have to hide her face, just her strength, and she has to do so with care. If the DarkWalker sees her, he'll come for her, a hero to the rescue, and she'll never get away.

It's a good glamour, as good as she can manage under the circumstances. She leaves her cocoon and the side of the river. There's an old house nearby, haunted by a ghost, owned by an EMT currently on duty, so she sneaks in easily and calms the dog with her whispers. She finds keys for the old sports car in the driveway, a muscle car in need of work, but it's sufficient for her needs. She drives south, away from 30 and away from the facility and away from Jack Harlow.

She'd liked him. She'd even trusted him. She can't anymore. She's not stupid. He's unstable. He's dangerous. The anger seething inside him needs an outlet, and she won't risk being it.

She doesn't have to go far. Just a dozen miles through the snakelike Pennsylvania roads, she reaches a Giant grocery store. Inside, she selects certain herbs.

Grocery store herbs aren't necessarily the kind of quality she needs to spell casting, but they'll suffice. She does better in the produce aisle, finding fresh ingredients and, for a snack, a pair of oranges. She also finds a cheap paring knife, which is all she needs at the moment. Her own knives are inaccessible, but not forever. No one stops her when she walks out with her ingredients.

In the lot behind the store, alone, she eats the oranges first. They're juicy and sweet and make her hands sticky, which is all part of the spell. They're invigorating, too, and refreshing, and she's already beginning to feel better. She spreads salt around her and other spices, and cuts open the green and red vegetables. She recites words in her native tongue, Haitian Creole, which flow from her with unimaginable ease and comfort. She almost feels like she's home again, though of course home is a place she'd never return to under any circumstances. But the ideal of home has never left her.

She performs the ritual and opens a portal and confirms it's free from contamination, then she walks through. In this way, she escapes Pennsylvania, Jack Harlow, and his father's organization.

She's at a small lake with a fountain. This has never been a place she called home, but she knows people here and that gives her some sense of comfort. Again with the comfort. She's been on the edge of the unknown for too long. She wants *akasan*, or at the very least milk and cinnamon.

She walks through the city streets, away from the lake and into the downtown area, to Orange Avenue and to the jazz bar where she first met the DarkWalker. The bouncer gives her a onceover and disapproves of the state of her. So does she. He allows her in anyhow. There's no line. It's too early in the night for a crowd. She has no idea what day of the week, but the sun's only set within the past hour or two.

At the table where she expects to see him, the vaudoux sits surrounded by his entourage of sycophants and bodyguards and minor powers. He chases some away with a wave of his hand. The big men in their suits and bulging muscles do not go far. The women dance with each other on the dancefloor in front of the stage where a band of some sort is setting up. Naomi takes a seat at the edge of the booth.

The vaudoux smiles. It's a big, bright smile against his dark skin. He says, "So you have seen something, have you?"

Naomi does not smile. She says, simply, "*Wi.*" It's the language of home. One of the vaudoux's supplicants returns with a rum drink of some sort. At first, she ignores it. But as she tells her story, as she tells Jack Harlow's story, she drinks three of them.

3.

In one of the Land Rovers, between the Susquehanna and Manhattan, Lance interrupts Jack Harlow's thoughts. "You can stop now, you know."

"I can't."

"You can. You can go back to the road. You can leave me on the side of the road."

"You can leave any time," Jack tells him.

In the back seat, Colton and Eulalia are silent. The warlock may even be asleep, or as close as he can get in his condition. He won't be fully recovered when they reach the Brownstone, but he will be able to fight.

"They assigned me to be your handler," Lance tells him, "and they ran a mission under me without my knowledge."

"Are you saying you're in this fight, too?"

"I'm saying, it's my job to help you consider your options."

"There's no back," Jack Harlow tells him. "There's no place to go back to."

"You know Naomi's safe. She escaped."

"And Nick Hunter?" Jack asks. The vampire hunter, the *former* vampire hunter, went east, to Richmond, rather than north, and though he's still doing the things he's always done, he's not the man he was. "Someone has to pay for that."

"The Ravens," Lance says, "is an organization, not a person." After a brief pause, he adds, "Those were people you killed, or had killed, back there."

Jack doesn't respond to this. He turns back to the window, to watch the woods as they drive through the night. There's nothing to see, not really, except he sees more deeply and more thoroughly than he used to. One of the skills he acquired in the shallow city. His strength, his resilience – everything is changing, everything is growing. He reaches further than he used to, and he gains more by doing so. He senses creatures near and far: ghosts and revenants, some as old as the Susquehanna and Delaware and Montauk and Munsee, some as recent as the Amish and Mennonite, a wanderer and a hitchhiker; but also beasts like the wendigo and a satyr and a family of devils; and at least one practitioner of pow wow magic powerful enough to glow like a nova.

They're still hours from Manhattan. Jack would drive faster, but he'd be in his Mustang and he'd be alone, and while his immunity has generally protected him even from police, it would not stop him from hitting a turn too fast in the Pennsylvania countryside and wrecking in the trees or against a brick house or a cornfield or a graveyard.

From the back, Eulalia asks, "Can we get water?"

Jack turns to look at her. She's so small, so quiet, so different than the woman she'd been under the mine. There, she was a servant to the queen underground; here, she's just a scarred and scared woman in a world she knows nothing about.

"Next place," Lance says. "We need fuel."

"You don't have to come with me," Jack reminds her. He doesn't want to make anyone come with him, not when he doesn't know what will happen. He's not prophetic, at least not yet, but he senses an ending of sorts coming closer, not just coming but barreling uncontrolled and unstoppably. It might just be the end of this Order of the White Ravens, but it feels bigger than that. Because he's explored them, he's reached through the threads of them, tangled though they may be. He hasn't mastered such talents, but he finds much bravado and little substance. Only a handful of watchers worked out of the Susquehanna facility; the rest were hired, no better than mercenaries, and many of them would likely move on to a new assignment should the paychecks stop. At the top of this web: Jack's father, Jonathan Harlow.

Oh, there are other threads, and other names, should Jack push hard enough to find them. But there's a Council, and his father's a part of it, an influential voice, which somehow makes no sense because he's also leading a hidden faction within the Ravens.

"Vermillion," Jack says aloud.

Lance reacts as if slapped. "What?"

"A name I keep finding," Jack says. "My father's involved. What are they?"

"A legend," Lance tells him. "A story." The Land Rover seems to shudder when he sighs. "I suppose it's not, is it?"

"Tell me about it."

"There were spiders, once," Lance says, "according to the files, who worked with the order. They had their own agenda, presumably."

"Which was?"

"To cement their station in life?" Lance says. It sounds like a question. He clearly doesn't know the details. He's not well-versed in his White Raven history. "They controlled some of the watchers. There was a war." He hesitates. "A battle. The Vermillion were wiped out. The watchers had too much knowledge, could unleash too much raw power."

"When?" Jack asks.

"A thousand years ago? Two?" Lance shakes his head. "It might've happened twice. I don't remember."

"Why would you remember?" Eulalia asks. "You weren't there."

Jack looks at her again. She's doesn't seem to be full of mysteries, but she most certainly is.

"Neither were you," Lance points out.

"I'm older than I look."

"You're human," Jack tells her.

"I earned each of these scars," she tells him.

Jack smiles. He sees it now. Each scar, each individual line of the mishmash of her face and presumably body, gave her – what, another lifetime? He asks, "What do you know about Vermillion?"

"Actually," she says, "I thought it was a drug."

Jack has no idea what she's talking about, but Lance says, "That's Scarlet."

"I forget," Eulalia says, trailing off and looking out the window. She says the next words so quietly, it's doubtful anyone in all of creation hears them except for Jack. "I haven't forgotten *everything*."

Ahead, there's a Sheetz gas station. Lance pulls the Land Rover into it. In the back, Colton opens his eyes. Eulalia, with the door already open, says, "I'll get you some water."

She goes inside. Lance, outside, starts pumping gas into the truck, leaving Jack Harlow alone with Colton. The warlock, still leaning back, says, "You changed down there. More than I realized."

"I haven't changed," Jack says. "I just know who I am now."

"That," Colton says, "is a change most of us never manage to make."

The night grows suddenly darker. The air goes chill. Colton leans forward and Jack leans back. He's used to encountering random things at random places. This is nothing new to him. The warlock, maybe, has never seen the modern world, maybe doesn't even know about cars except through the stories of creatures that came down from above. Jack's not sure how long, if at all, the warlock lived outside of the mine.

"Trouble," Colton says.

"I'm still enough of a watcher," Jack says, "that it should ignore me, whatever it is."

"If you're that much a watcher," Colton says, "shouldn't you know what it is?"

The gas station lights flicker and go out. Clouds obscure the stars and the moon. For a moment, there's not a shred of light to be found beyond the Land Rover's dashboard. Then there's a flash of lightning, a distant bolt but bright and flickering, revealing legions of gray, mottled faces in the darkness, yellow teeth, eyes so white they hurt to see. The afterimage of these soldiers - and that's what they are, soldiers, armed with lances and maces and spears and swords, hardened and well-tested soldiers wearing the teeth of their enemies in chains around their necks and dangling from their ears and surgically embedded into their knuckles to give their punches bite. They don't surround the Land Rover or the gas station, not exactly, though they're everywhere and deep in every direction, but they all face west, providing Jack Harlow and the warlock with views of them from all sides.

In the next moment, in the total darkness that follows the flash of lightning, as the thunder rolls through, Jack experiences a moment of blindness, a moment in which he cannot see by any means, not through his eyes and not through his soul, and not through whatever new senses have awakened within him.

Light returns, all the electricity suddenly restored. Colton whistles in some form of appreciation rooted in dread. The driver side doors open, and both Lance and Eulalia climb back in. They've got water and chocolate for everyone, and start handing it out as if nothing happened. "It's amazing in there," Eulalia's saying. "They've got hot dogs." Clearly, she's never had one before, but she's got one now wrapped in aluminum foil, and she's never seemed more childlike. The smell of onions and relish and mustard on top of it are nearly overwhelming. The creatures, the legion of soldiers, are gone, and were never actually there.

Colton puts a hand on Jack's shoulder from the seat behind him and says, "Not all futures are immediate."

Jack shakes himself loose of the vision. He bites into the chocolate without tasting it, swallows half a bottle of water without taking a breath. Colton adds, "Visions are tricky things, you know. They're rarely precise, often symbolic, usually incomprehensible."

But Jack Harlow, DarkWalker, understands the nature of this vision. It's not some faraway distant prophecy. They're headed toward it now, in this Land Rover, possibly at the end of this road or at least the end of this journey. Whatever waits in Manhattan, it will not be easy.

4.

Even in the hour before dawn, getting into New York City is obnoxious. Jack Harlow's glad he's not driving. He'd probably do something foolish, like bringing down fire and hail, that would attract all the wrong kinds of attention. He's not actually sure he can bring fire or hail, but he doesn't want to test himself. He doesn't know what he's capable of anymore. Instead, he watches the other cars, the taxis and buses, the people rushing up from the subways, the mechanics that keep the city running. Every person is a piece of that machinery, and every piece is replaceable.

Eventually, Lance reaches a garage and parks the Land Rover next two three others of the same year and color. Must've been a group discount. Then it's a short walk, the four of them side by side under what had once been gaslights. Jack sees the echoes of them even now.

They reach the Brownstone. There's a door under the wide stoop, but they climb the seven steps to the front door. Lance rings the buzzer.

"Are you known here?" Jack asks.

Lance says, "Yes."

The door opens – only the three inches the chain will allow, and a uniformed man looks out from between the crack.

"Lance Turner, handler," Lance says, "bringing in the watcher Jack Harlow for debrief."

That's not exactly true, hardly true at all, but the man accepts the information with a nod. He closes the door, undoes the chain, and opens it again.

The foyer is opulent, all rich, deep woods, a coat rack, a crystal chandelier. Double doors hide a room to the right. Beyond those, stairs go up, big comfortable stairs unlike what Jack usually imagines for New York. The hallway is wider, too. The Brownstone is old. In its day, it was elegant, and it remains so, even if the ghost of its former self would outshine its current face. The hall past the stairs leads to another room, to which the man takes them. It stretches further, presumably to a kitchen considering the scents of maple, fresh bread, and cinnamon wafting down the hall.

The man opens the double doors to this room and precedes them by a single step. His announcement is succinct and to the point. "The DarkWalker."

It's a big room, a huge room, an office furnished with a pair of desks and a large globe and bookshelves. Paintings hang on the wall, real paintings, centuries-old cracked oils painted by masters. Jack thinks he even recognizes one. The rug in here is primarily red and bigger than most rooms he's ever slept in.

Straight ahead, the main desk is a boat, or a tank, and a large woman with small eyes sits behind it. Her eyes hide everything. They're impossible to see, impossible to read, even for Jack, and they're unquestionably focused on him.

"Would you see the others to the Front Room," the woman says. It should sound like a question, but it doesn't.

"They're with me," Jack says.

"They're unnecessary," the woman says.

"Thank you, Ma'am," Lance says, nearly bowing as he retreats from the room. Eulalia offers Jack a weak smile. Colton seems resigned to anything. A moment later, the man closes the door, leaving Jack alone in the big office with the big woman. He steps forward, toward a red leather chair in front of the desk. Another half dozen chairs, all yellow upholstery and wood, and a richly upholstered chaise are scattered unassumingly throughout the room.

"Please, sit," the woman says. "My name is Diana Walcott. I've been waiting for you."

Jack takes his time approaching the desk. He looks about the room, noticing the titles on the bookshelves – *The Book of Lost Fates, The Necronomicon, The Bohemian-American Cookbook, The Book of Thoth,* Poe, Wilde, Blavatsky, Harry Houdini's *The Right Way to Do Wrong* – and he notices the other keepsakes and trophies, as well – a candle in the shape of a gargoyle, an ornate silver teaspoon, ivory dice, a crystal skull, a deck of handmade playing cards with a Joker showing on top, an iron key.

"Acquisitions," Diana Walcott says. "From my various expeditions. I've done a fair bit of traveling in my day. I'm afraid I'm old now, and generally confined to this Brownstone."

Nothing of New York City reaches into this office, not a sound, not a hint. It's well-insulated, fortified, protected, even soundproofed. Jack approves. He sits in the chair, all the way back, sinking in to what may be the most comfortable seat he's ever imagined. "You're a watcher," Jack says.

She smiles. "I think we're well beyond that, don't you?"

Jack stops looking about the room and looks directly at Diana Walcott, at those beady eyes that reveal nothing, at the blue makeup around her eyes and the slightly garish red lipstick, the set of gold rings on her hand and the band of obsidian she wears in place of a wedding ring.

She presses a button under her desk. In a moment, the man returns with a tray carrying a bottle of beer and two glasses – one for beer, one for liquor. He sets the beer glass and bottle on the desk, then turns to Jack and asks, "What's your pleasure?"

"It's only just dawn," Jack tells him.

The man doesn't respond, simply waits for Jack's instructions. There's a side table with an assortment of whiskeys and brandies and gins. Jack says, "Milk."

The man nods and exits. Diana's pouring her beer. "It's been a long day," she tells him. "We lost one of our facilities last night."

"I know."

She gives him a smile that says she knows.

"The Council made a mistake," Diana tells him as she waits for the head of the beer to retreat. "I tell you I was outvoted only to explain why I'm here now to speak with you."

"Rather than one of the others?"

"Their fear is, I believe, justified."

The man returns with the same tray, but the glass has been replaced by something more appropriate for the milk it contains. Jack takes the glass and holds the milk up to his lips as though he's about to drink, and he can detect nothing wrong with it.

"You're not afraid?" Jack asks.

"You're angry, but not with me," she tells him. "They thought it would be best to contain you."

"How many are on the Council?"

"That's a secret."

"Seven?" Jack asks. "No, eight. One doesn't vote, merely oversees."

She smiles again. "You got that from me?"

Jack skips the question. "You – I'm sorry, your Council, believed the mine at Silver Blade was appropriate?"

"They did."

"Isn't the mine a death sentence?"

Diana lifts her beer and drains the glass. She wipes her mouth with a handkerchief. She says, "Essentially."

"But you didn't know what was going on inside, did you?" Jack asks. "The residents of the shallow city were readying to revolt."

Diana laughs. It's short and absent of humor. "They were always on the verge of open rebellion. Not everyone realized the catalyst you would be."

"And now, what?" Jack asks. "You think you want to bring me in?"

She laughs again and shakes her head. "No, Mr. Harlow," she says. "We expect you to destroy us. We're going to save you the trouble."

"What?"

"The Order of the White Raven has existed for approximately eighteen hundred years. Over that time, we've watched the darkest portals, we've kept the most hideous beasts at bay, and we've tracked the oncoming dangers. But in recent years, our numbers have dwindled, and the numbers in the darkness have dwindled, and it seemed we were all but ready to die. Then you came along, the DarkWalker, the first DarkWalker in over three hundred years. And you ripped open a portal to Hell."

Jack waits for her to continue. He was there, on Long Island, just a month ago.

"In the past twelve hours, the Order of the White Raven has disavowed all of its operatives, relinquished the strongholds in Shanghai, Prague, and Casablanca, and released all of its hired soldiers."

He waits for more, but she seems to think she's done.

"You're not telling me everything," Jack says. "*Vermillion.*"

Diana draws a deep, long breath, and says, "Yes, well, there is that, is there not?"

"The organization within the organization," Jack says.

"Symbolized by the tiger, yes," Diana says. Not spider, he notices.

"My father lied to me," Jack says. "He said he was part of an organization within, but he was always part of all of it."

"Jonathan Harlow sits on the Council. Everything he's done has been sanctioned."

"He's Vermillion."

"He is indeed."

"And you knew? The rest of you?"

"Of course. The watchers serve a purpose, Mr. Harlow, but Vermillion serves another purpose. A more active role, you might say. Instead of just watching, instead of merely recording and analyzing information, they act on what we learn. They act from within, but in secret, because sometimes the dangers to this world are enormous and there's no one else to do the work."

"I'm sure I'm missing something," Jack says.

"The Order of the White Raven has been dissolved," Diana says. "Your anger no longer has a target, Mr. Harlow. You can kill me, if you wish, but I'm an old woman and I'm not going to survive the day under any circumstances."

Jack almost lets that by. He almost misses it. "Not going to survive the *day*?"

Diana Walcott smiles. It's the ugliest thing Jack's ever seen. She smiles, and sits back in her chair, and presses her button to ring for more beer. Jack sees it now, the trace of poison in the glass. He smells it on her breath, and sees it in the whites of her eyes. The man returns with a tray and another bottle of beer and a fresh glass. "As I said, Mr. Harlow. It's been a long night."

She doesn't need a second glass of beer to kill herself. It's already done. It's not fast-acting, but it won't be long. From the looks of it, it won't be unpleasant.

"Why?" Jack asks.

"I've outlived my purpose, Mr. Harlow." She smiles, and she lifts the beer glass, but her hand is unsteady. She spills some, and does her best to bite back her disappointment with herself. "And so has the Order. We cannot protect the world from what's next."

"What's next? What can't you protect the world from?"

"You mean, besides you?" Diana Walcott smiles. Her eyes are glazing over. She sets the glass down unfinished because she can't hold it any longer. "Armies have amassed under the kings at Armageddon, Mr. Harlow."

5.

For a while, Jack Harlow, DarkWalker, sits alone in the big office with the corpse of the Councilwoman. He leans back in the red leather chair and considers how much of what she's said is true, how much is meant to mislead him, what he can even do with that information.

If the watchers are no more, Vermillion still exists. He's not done. His father's out there somewhere. So is his sister. They were both part of it, and they wouldn't have thrown away their lives for – well, for nothing. Diana Walcott is dead, she's dead for no good reason, and she's dead by her own hand. Why? Fear? Fear of him, Jack Harlow, and the retribution he intended to deliver?

Eventually, Jack gets up. He examines the objects on the desk, a calendar book with all appointments – every one after this meeting with Jack Harlow, which was scribbled quickly by pencil – are blacked out, past and future. There's one listed for 10 this morning, but Diana had gone through the entire book with a Sharpie and made them unreadable.

There's a collection of beer bottle caps in the top drawer, an assortment of pens and pencils, a small jar with spare change, a bottle of ink, a ring of keys that presumably lock every door in this Brownstone. In the other drawers, he finds a book, an Oliveri 9mm handgun, a bottle of Dewar's, a ledger with coded entries, a 1980s era HP scientific calculator, a yellowed manuscript of *The Book of the Dead*, another manuscript with colorful illustrations but a title in Latin calligraphy that's beyond Jack's immediate understanding – because it, like the ledger, is written in code and only looks like Latin.

There's only one file, a thin manila folder. *DarkCrawler.*

Jack presses the button to summon the man. He appears at the doorway wearing a shield of solemnity over his face.

"What's your name?" Jack asks.

"Frederick."

"Frederick, is there anyone else in this Brownstone?"

"Your friends, sir."

"You don't have to call me sir."

"Of course not."

"Can you...?" Jack gestures toward the corpse in the chair.

"Of course, sir," Frederick says. "Will that be all?"

"We'll need breakfast before our ten o'clock," Jack says.

For a moment, Jack's not sure how Frederick will respond to that. It seems a basic request, and if Jack's feeling hungry the others must be starved. There's some internal battle taking place, and Jack doesn't want to interfere, but it doesn't last long. "If you and your friends will be in the dining room in sixty minutes, sir."

"Thank you, Frederick."

The man nods. It's as close as he'll get to saying *You're welcome.*

There's a set of double doors connecting the office to what is presumably the Front Room. Jack opens it and finds a series of couches, a phonograph, encyclopedias and fiction books all a century old or more, and Lance, Eulalia, and Carlton.

There's a coffee table between them. Jack drops the file onto it. "There's work to be done," he says. "I don't know what, exactly, but we're to do it."

"What did you learn?" Colton asks.

Jack smiles. "Her name was Diana Walcott."

"*Was?*" Eulalia asks. "She was an old lady."

"Not by my hand," Jack says. "We'll have a visitor at 10, and we'll have breakfast in an hour. If we can find the dining room."

"What did you *learn?*" Colton asks again.

"The Order of the White Raven has been dissolved," Jack says. "She also said something about Armageddon."

"The end of the world?" Colton asks.

"No," Lance says. "The mountain."

"I don't believe she meant it literally," Jack says.

Lance shakes his head. "I wouldn't be so sure she didn't."

"We may have another problem," Jack says, pointing to the file. "That's not about me."

"What's a DarkCrawler?" Eulalia asks.

Lance is still shaking his head as he picks up the file. It's thin, because no one really knows the answer. He skims through the three pages – that's all there is, not even a photo or illustration, and mostly white space – and says, "This file's only four months old."

"Look again," Jack says. "You're familiar with my file, right?"

"Of course." Lance glances again, and the moment he sees it, his expression changes. "That's the same day you stood in the field."

Stood in the field is a strange way of saying *You stood against vampires and demons and harpies and wraiths and zombies and other dead things, you and your friend the vampire hunter and the vampire Jia Li and your lover, Lisa Sparrow, the love of your life, who died later that very same night trying to save not just you but the world.* Jack merely nods.

"I don't trust coincidences," Lance says.

"Neither do I."

"What does it say?" Colton asks.

"It says, basically, there's a creature out there ripping its way through the darkness, destroying everything it can get its hands on." Lance pauses for a moment, for dramatic effect or because he's not certain he believes what he's about to say. "And *acquiring* their talents."

"Acquiring?" Colton looks uncertain.

Looking at Jack, Eulalia says, "Like you."

Everyone looks at Jack. Even Jack looks at Jack. Finally, he says, "*Not* like me." He pauses, because he's not entirely sure of everything. "I think I've been gaining strength and power and, as you said, *talent*, by proximity. Everyone thought I was a watcher for so long because I grew up in a family of watchers. I absorbed their abilities and duplicated them, and I never knew I was anything else."

"You started to know," Lance says. "I've read your file."

Jack shakes his head. "I didn't care, I never cared, so I never examined it. Not until you sent me into the mines." Lance averts his eyes when he says it, but Jack continues. "Was it a test, to see how much I would absorb?"

"Your time in Hell," Lance says.

Jack shakes his head. "Untested. Unrealized. It was all just potential there."

"What happened in Silver Blade that changed you?" Lance asks.

"The pit," Eulalia says, referring to where her mistress, the seer, had ordered Jack tossed.

"Below the pit, below the Shallow City, and below the Deep City," Jack says, and he hesitates because he's not used to sharing so much. "I met the original DarkWalker."

CHAPTER FOUR

JOHN URBANCIK

1.

Frederick serves breakfast in a dining room big enough to serve the Russian army. The plates are real china, the silverware real silver, the food real good. Frederick brings it in waves, fresh fruits and plain yogurt and nuts, steaming biscuits and apple butter, scrambled eggs and sausage, pancakes and maple syrup, three different juices and strong coffee. The meal is almost enough to break them out of their silence.

Jack Harlow sits at the head of the table as though this is his house. Frederick had insisted in his quiet way, and put Lance Turner to his right, Eulalia to his left, Colton beside her. They make good work of the food, and it's the most delicious meal any of them remembers eating. The thin *DarkCrawler* file is on the table in the Front Room, Diana Walcott's corpse has been removed from the office, and it's almost like a real, functioning household. It's exactly the kind of household Jack Harlow has never known, though Lance seems perfectly comfortable in this environment.

During the meal, they talk about nothing that matters, and Jack doesn't talk at all. Eulalia says something about the last time she saw fresh fruit. Colton thanks Frederick, enthusiastically, twice. Lance admit he's never eaten at this Brownstone before.

When it's all done and Frederick has cleared the table and only coffee remains, Jack Harlow breaks his silence. "We're not done."

"The rescue," Colton says, "is over."

"You're welcome to leave," Jack says. "I apparently have an appointment in thirty minutes, and there's still the matter of Vermillion."

"Vermillion," Lance says, rolling the word around in his mouth. "I never believed in them."

"I'll meet with whoever's coming," Jack says. "Lance, I'd like you in the office with me."

"I'll hide, of course," Eulalia says.

"There are two more floors in this Brownstone, and rooms to be explored," Jack says. "I expect the two of you to find whatever needs finding. Are there more bodies? More residents of any sort? I want to know. Who lived here? Is there a *DarkWalker* file? Anything on Lizzie." He catches himself. "Elizabeth Harlow. Or Jonathon Harlow." He doesn't go further, but he wants to know more about his mom. It's hard to believe he knows so little about her. He'd lived in her house for most of eighteen years. What other secrets does his family keep?

Eulalia nods and smiles. She has no wish to be displayed as a trophy and warning anymore. The past decades – how long? – have almost been too much for her to bear. Jack can see the weight of it all in her eyes. She's older even than she'd admit.

Colton rises first. "Right," he says. "There's work to do."

Jack Harlow rings the bell – he's not used to summoning servants – and when Frederick arrives, he says, "We're expecting a guest."

"Yes, sir."

"We'll be in the office."

"Of course, sir."

Jack hesitates. He asks, "Do you know who we're expecting?"

"Of course not, sir." He's lying. Of course he's lying. He's still loyal to the Order, perhaps to Diana Walcott. The man has always been a household servant, and comes from a long line of household servants. What might he have been instead?

"We'll be in the office," Jack says again.

Lance takes the chair at the other desk, which is as big as the mahogany monstrosity Jack sits behind. From this vantage point, he sees the room differently. He sees the invisible threads binding pieces of art and sculpture. He sees points of light on the globe, little winks of red and yellow and green. A safe in the wall contains untold secrets. He hadn't even noticed it before. He goes to it now. Since his time in Orlando, locks have been complaint for him. He probably caught the skill from Nick Hunter without realizing it. He spins the dial, listens to the clicks, admits he has no fundamental knowledge of the mechanics of locks, and convinces the safe to open anyhow.

Inside, there's money. Piles of petty cash in tens, twenties, and fifties. Credit cards in a variety of names. A stack of passports from numerous countries, including several in the name of Diana Walcott. Another Oliveri, this one a heavy .50 caliber. Another ledger indicating amounts taken from, and returned to, the petty cash.

"I thought there might be files here," Jack says.

"There's a file room in the basement," Lance says, "but those will only be active and open files. Most are kept at a place called The Mountain."

Jack shakes his head. "Armageddon again?"

"I believe," Lance says, "it's in Colorado."

Jack's never been to Colorado. He's always stuck to the east coast. He doesn't know anything west of the Mississippi. To be honest, he doesn't know the Mississippi, either.

"Do you have a guess as to who's coming?" Lance asks.

Jack glances at the clock. Ten minutes. "Only guesses."

"It's a recently made appointment," Lance says. "Look at the way it was written. The same pencil that was used to write you in this morning."

"I can't believe she had to pencil me in," Jack says.

"And she spent some time last night blacklining everything else," Lance says. He's got the calendar book in front of him.

"Another show for my benefit?"

"Someone like Diana Walcott, she was born into secrets," Lance says. "She wrapped them around herself, consumed them. She used them well, and they made her powerful. Secrets died with her, terrible and horrible secrets."

"Armageddon?"

"No," Lance says. Then he corrects himself. "I don't think so. She may have known things I don't, that no one does, but anyone can read the Bible."

"I haven't," Jack says.

"It's symbolic," Lance says. "*Then they gathered the kings together to the place that in Hebrew is called Armageddon.*"

"That's it?" Jack asks.

"There are other references," Lance says, "but that's the first, and the only one in the Bible. I may have misquoted it."

"Revelations."

"Yes." The doorbell rings.

Jack walks around the side of his desk and sits in Diana Walcott's oversized chair. "The end of the world."

"An end of the world," Lance says. "We're almost always facing an end of some sort." He drops the calendar onto his desk. "But if Diana Walcott said it, if those were her last words, it's got to mean something."

"A clue to this appointment?"

"I doubt it," Lance says. He leans back in his chair, which moves with him. "I have a guess, and you're not going to like it."

Frederick appears from the door to the hall to announce their visitor. "Elizabeth Harlow."

She strides past the servant, raises her arm, and aims a Colt Peacemaker right at Jack Harlow.

2.

In the next moment, Jack Harlow notices everything.

He hears Lizzie say, "Walcott," because obviously that's who she expects.

He hears her pull the trigger. He hears the explosion of the gunshot. How could he not?

He sees the smile on Frederick's face. It's the first suggestion of real emotion, satisfaction at a plan well-made and well-executed.

Lance's face goes through a series of emotions like a contortionist. Jack can't read it all, can't interpret it, not in the moment.

He feels the bullet rip through his chest. It's to the left of his heart, punctures his lung, burns straight through and out his back. The pain is instant and total. His whole body shuts down with it. He's thrown backwards, even in the chair, and spins off to the left. He falls in slow motion. He's not dead, not yet, but the next breath doesn't happen, and he's spitting blood, and it's hard to know any of this past the pain. He hits the wood floor face first and twists so that he's on his side. There's movement elsewhere in the Brownstone. There's no sound anymore through the echo of that thunder. There's no sensation anymore besides white hot agony. He tries to take another breath, but it's hopeless. He doesn't have the strength to pick himself up. He manages to land on his back.

Lizzie's to him first. She's kneeling. She's still got the Peacemaker in her hand. Whatever she's saying, it's hard to register. "I didn't realize." Maybe. "It doesn't matter." Probably not. "Just as good." Then she leans closer, whispers directly into his ear, words that make it through the cacophony of all his other senses. "I'm glad it was me."

Jack Harlow, DarkWalker, closes his eyes, cutting off at least one source of chaos, and slips into instinct.

3.

   Jack Harlow doesn't expect to open his eyes again. He expects Hell, or some variation, one of the many versions he's seen. He doesn't know how it's decided, where a person goes when they die, if they remain as a ghost or something else. He has no expectations. And no fears. He hopes he'll go someplace great, someplace divine, someplace very unlike the hells he's already seen, but he doubts that. He's not always been a good man. Often, he's been indifferent, uninspired, a quiet drifter and witness to horrors he couldn't prevent. He's not sure he's a good man now. He's angry and frustrated and tired of being lied to. He's done with the manipulations. He wants to be reunited with Lisa Sparrow. He saw a future with her, a regular normal everyday future, the kind available to almost anyone else. He's not a regular, normal, or everyday person. He knows this isn't his future anymore. She died, she risked her life to save his and she lost, and if he's being totally honest, one hundred percent truthful, and completely real, he blames himself. More than anyone or anything else. Not the imp. Not the demon. None of that, none of them, would've happened if he hadn't stepped out of the shadows at *The Precipice*, just a random club in what could've been any city, and changed the course of both their lives. This knowledge hurts more than the bullet.

4.

But Jack Harlow is a DarkWalker, and as such he's been slowly absorbing the powers and strengths of the creatures he's been exposed to. For most of twenty years, he was in the presence of watchers, his family, three of them at least and probably others who came in and out of the house. He's not immune to the darkness like he seemed to be, and he's certainly not impervious to lead, but he's not without an incredible store of resources beyond even his knowledge.

He opens his eyes. Reaches up at his sister's throat.

Her eyes go wide.

The pain returns when Jack opens his eyes. It's like he's reclaimed consciousness and all that goes with it. Lizzie grabs at his wrist, but she might as well try to stop a runaway railroad car. He squeezes. He sees her veins, her arteries, the blood that is her life, and he knows she'll make a good donor. He's lost much. He's not even thinking, not really, just letting instinct guide him. He pulls her neck down to him and bites. Rips. Tears. Drinks.

It's not a long drink. Just enough to calm his pain, to cool the heat, to ease the flow of blood. He's not a vampire. But he's been close to vampires, intimate with one, and he's gained something of their strength.

Lizzie can't speak through the fingers around her windpipe, but he hears her thoughts, or what might be thoughts. Appeals. Fears. Desires. She's glad she shot him, glad she eliminated this threat, glad she was able to save the world and – and her daughter? She has a daughter? When did that happen?

But she's also thankful he's the one to kill her. The world is hard. She's never had it easy, even when she absolutely did, even when everything was handed to her. She's unintelligible in the end, images of her daughter, Jack's niece – Rowan, her name is Rowan. He's not exactly a mind reader, he doesn't think, but all of this pours out of her like blood.

He pushes her away.

The wound in her neck is worse than the wounds in his chest and back. Inside, the holes in his lung are repairing themselves, able to do so because of the influx of fresh blood. He tastes his sister's blood in his mouth. It's not coppery like he'd expected, but sweet, like cotton candy, and sticky. It leaves a bitter aftertaste in his mouth.

When he looks up, his sister is dying and Lance Turner is cradling her head in his lap. There are tears in his eyes, not tears for Jack Harlow, no. And when Lance looks at Jack, rage seethes behind his eyes.

There's still a great deal of pain. Jack's still weak, far from recovered. He hears something in the background, a noise from the far end of the room, but he's not able to focus there yet. He has Lance directly in front of him. He manages to say, "You...have a daughter?" Lance doesn't respond, not immediately, not in any way that matters. Lizzie Harlow, Elizabeth now, Elizabeth perhaps for years now, expels her last breath. Her eyes glaze over. Jack sees the life leave her, but not her soul, her spirit, or whatever remains. She's just gone.

The moment is unbearably long. Lance rocks her and cries and looks away from Jack, looks anywhere and everywhere else. There are voices, but they don't register.

Jack says, "That wasn't supposed to happen."

Lance focuses on Jack. If he'd had power behind his eyes, they would sear through Jack, body and soul. "Of course it wasn't." Through gritted teeth. But what was supposed to happen? Did Lizzie come here intending to shoot Diana Walcott?

"I didn't mean..."

"It doesn't matter what you meant," Lance says.

"She was my sister."

"She was *my* love."

Jack closes his eyes. This isn't surrender, he's not retreating from the pain or the words. But he knows exactly how Lance feels right now. He knows it, and can feel the emotions emanating from him. He's felt them – still feels them – himself. He's never gotten over the loss of Lisa Sparrow. He likely never will.

"I hate to say so," Colton says, breaking through the moment from the other side of the desk, "but we have another problem to deal with. Frederick."

Jack looks. Colton holds Frederick by the scruff of his neck. A faint orangey scent lingers, something magical. Frederick is grinning, but the grin is fading and being replaced by a scowl and it's not at all pleasant to look at.

Jack doesn't get up, doesn't bother to say anything at all.

"He tried to make a call," Colton says.

Eulalia holds up the mobile phone as if presenting proof.

"And I rather liked the man," Colton says. "Can I kill him?"

"Can you make him talk?"

5.

They – Jack Harlow, Eulalia, and Colton – bring Frederick to the basement, which is a series of rooms including his own, but the main room has a few chairs and a billiard table and concrete walls. It will suffice for their intentions. They sit Frederick in the big chair, practically a throne, and Colton goes upstairs to the kitchen to gather ingredients.

"Just so we're clear," Jack tells Frederick, "I haven't decided whether or not you die."

Frederick keeps his head bowed and his eyes cast downward. He says nothing and does nothing.

"I wasn't always like this," Jack tells him. "Used to be, I'd just walk away. But lately, I haven't been allowed to do that. Do you know why that is?"

Frederick says, "I serve the Order."

"I'm all that's left of the Order," Jack tells him.

"*Rogue.*" Frederick spits it out like a curse. It's not the first time the word's been used to describe Jack. It's practically meaningless.

"So," Jack says, "you will decide for me." The truth is, Jack can talk but not much else. He needs more time to recover, or a spell from Colton, or another dose of fresh blood. But he's not a vampire; he doesn't need it to survive. He's a lot of things, actually, all wrapped up together, vampire among them, but he lacks the restrictions and limitations of any of them. "Do you want to die, Frederick?"

Frederick glances up, meets Jack's eyes, and the answer is there. He's resigned to death. He's done. He's seen as much as he needs to see. He's played his role and is ready to walk offstage.

"Fine," Jack says. "I'll see to it myself. But not until after our little chat."

"Are you up to this?" Eulalia asks. "You look pale."

"I am pale," Jack says, meaning it in a number of ways.

Colton comes downstairs carrying a drink on Frederick's tray. He offers it to their prisoner. It's a thick, milky amber with one large ice cube. "House special," Colton says.

Frederick takes the glass. He looks at it, looks at Jack, and throws the glass across the room. It shatters on the gray concrete wall. The milk oozes down the side.

"That," Jack says, "was not very polite."

Frederick mumbles. "I'm done with polite."

"I'm sorry, what was that?"

"I'm doing playing nice for you," Frederick says. "This is all your fault. Everything. You killed Mrs. Walcott."

"I believe that was you."

"You killed Ms. Harlow."

Jack doesn't bother responding to that, but it gets his pulse going.

"You created the DarkCrawler."

"I did no such thing," Jack says.

Frederick lifts his eyes, stares straight at Jack, anger and hatred bubbling within him and no longer under the surface. "And you're the DarkWalker. Everyone knows what that means."

"Enlighten me."

"Death. Suffering."

Jack considers this a moment. "Only for my enemies."

"You are the enemy of all of humanity."

Eulalia touches Jack's shoulder. "Perhaps you should let Colton prepare another serum."

"Oh, that wasn't a serum," Colton says. "The drink was meant to calm him, nothing more. The spell is cast. The words he says, they're the truth, as far as he knows it. He can say nothing else."

Frederick's gaunt, almost a ghost in his own right. He looks at Colton, the warlock, with unbridled disgust. "And you, your kind," he says. "Traitors to the race."

"And me?" Eulalia asks. "Have you got any pronouncements for the thousand year old human girl?"

He shifts his gaze again. "Only pity, for you. And contempt."

"I think I liked him better when he was quiet."

"Why did Diana Walcott kill herself?"

"The Council chose to disband."

"That means death?"

"Except for Vermillion, yes."

"And who is Vermillion?"

Frederick's grin is ugly and misshapen. "You know."

"My father."

"Jonathon Harlow."

"Where is he?" Jack asks.

The grin grows. "New York."

"City?"

Frederick doesn't respond.

"Is he in this Brownstone?" Jack asks.

"No, of course not. Why would he be here?"

"Vermillion has its own house?"

"Everyone has a house," Frederick says. "Even you."

"Do you want to die, Frederick?"

"No." Then: "Yes."

Jack glances at Colton. The warlock shrugs. "They can both be true."

"What would you like to do now, Frederick?" Jack asks. "The Order is disbanded. Where will you go?"

"To the grave."

"Any particular grave?"

He doesn't answer right away, because the answer is yes and he doesn't want to admit it.

"I'll make sure it happens," Jack tells him, leaning close. "Tell me where to find Vermillion House."

"You should be dead."

"I should be," Jack admits. "Several times over. But I'm not."

"There is no Vermillion House," Frederick says. "There's just an apartment."

"Where?"

Frederick's grin returns. "Here."

"He's not lying."

"We're not done searching," Eulalia says.

Jack glances to the basement ceiling, toward the office, where they'd left Lance Turner and the body of Jack's sister. "Check on Lance, would you?"

Eulalia hurries upstairs. Frederick, meanwhile, laughs. Under his breath. With amusement and derision.

6.

Lance is gone.

Lance and Lizzie's corpse are gone.

At first, Jack Harlow curses, and he does it well, delivering a stream of them in seven languages he doesn't even know. The office is empty except for the blood, his and his sister's. But that's enough to track her, isn't it? He can taste the scent of her blood in the air, the iron, the copper, in specific ratios different from Jack's blood. Though the two are mixed on the floor, they're also mixed on her corpse and, presumably, on Lance's hands. He won't get far.

"We should've..." Eulalia doesn't finish what she's about to say. They've left Colton downstairs with Frederick.

"He never went outside," Jack says.

"Upstairs, then?"

"Carrying a corpse?"

"There's an elevator."

There is. He hadn't noticed. It leads up, and there's not merely traces of blood scent inside, but streaks of it. It's in the hall and does not descend to the basement, but it does go up to the second, third, and fourth floors. A blood smear on the number three is suggestive.

There's room enough for two in the elevator. It's the fancy version of the elevator in the mineshaft at Silver Blade. It's opulent, heavily golden with large mirrors, and the accordion door adds to the art deco feel. It moves slowly, and Eulalia, behind Jack, isn't accustomed to riding in such things. She's not claustrophobic, but her heartrate has increased and her breaths come shallowly.

Jack doesn't bother to say anything.

They reach the third floor. Lance, in his flight, made no effort to obscure their path. Jack walks straight into the bedroom, into Lizzie's bedroom, where apparently she lives – lived – when at the Brownstone. Everything about the room says Lizzie, from the color choices to the pieces of art on the walls to the oversized mirror above the bureau. She lays, now, in the bed, amongst too many pillows and thick, fluffy coverlets and comforters. There's a lot of frill, a selection of expensive perfumes in fancy bottles on the bureau, and two chairs at a café table near the window. There, Lance sits, shrunken into himself, red eyes on Lizzie's corpse.

"You didn't even know her," Lance says.

"I did," Jack says. "Once."

"She didn't have to die."

"She didn't have to try to kill me."

"I'm not blaming you," Lance says. He wipes his face with the back of his hand. "But I saw what you did. You know what you did. You've gone beyond what you were, what you were meant to be. You *are* dangerous."

"I was always dangerous," Jack says. "Even when I didn't know it."

"It was a mistake, bringing you to Silver Blade," Lance says. "It was a mistake, contacting you at all. They should have left you to deal with your imp problem on your own. Maybe you would have died."

"Maybe," Jack says. "Probably."

Lance wipes his eyes again. He's not actively crying, not anymore, but there's something he can't clean away. "What happens to me now?"

Jack glances at Eulalia. She's not there to provide support, but he draws some from her anyway. She reminds him he was once human, or something close. "Rowan," Jack says. "My niece."

"My daughter."

Jack nods. "Where is she?"

"Home," Lance says. His throat fails him a moment. He manages to recover. "Upstate." That, too, isn't enough. "Sleepy Hollow."

"You should go home," Jack says.

Lance opens his mouth to argue, but thinks better of it.

"You should go home," Jack says again, "and do whatever needs to be done. You should forget about the Order, the watchers, the dark, and you should be Rowan's father."

At that, Lance sobs.

"There's money in the safe," Jack says. "Take what you need. Don't come back here." Jack takes a breath. "I never want to see you again. Under any circumstances. For any reason. Ever anywhere. Do you understand me? I want you to do for Rowan what my father, what Lizzie's father, was never able to do."

"She'd hate that, you know," Lance says. "She's always been Elizabeth."

Jack says, "Not always."

And that's all he has to say. There's nothing left. He turns and leaves the room. Eulalia lingers a moment, but there's nothing for her to say, either. There's a chance Lance Turner will come after Jack, maybe not today but some day in the future, seeking vengeance or justice or something.

As the elevator descends, Eulalia says, "You did a good thing, just now."

"No," Jack says. "I didn't. I condemned him to his knowledge."

7.

The Brownstone is bedrooms and parlors and a small library. The bedrooms are all big enough for beds and desks and chairs and tables, each with its own bathroom and closet, the master with a sitting room as big as any of the bedrooms. In the basement with Frederick again, Jack Harlow leans against the billiards table with his arms crossed. The man, the servant, slumps in the big chair. A line of sweat has formed on his forehead. His eyes are bloodshot. His fingers tremble with age as much as fear.

The basement contains the only apartment in the Brownstone, and it's Frederick's. There's a small living area and a bedroom, all meticulous and orderly. The bed's been made to military specifications, every sheet tucked tight, all in tan and beige and sand and chocolate. In the closet, there's a row of custom made suit jackets and crisp white dress shirts and black pants and three additional pairs of shoes and all the implements to clean, press, and mend all of it.

There's nothing to indicate an apartment occupied by Vermillion.

Which leaves Jack Harlow with an obvious conclusion. "The Brownstone," he says to Frederick. "It's the apartment you mean."

Frederick shakes his head. "I've given the Order everything."

"And now you'll give me this one last thing."

Frederick smiles. "No. The Brownstone is *not* the apartment."

Jack looks to Colton, but the warlock merely shrugs. "He can't lie, but that doesn't mean he has to tell us anything."

"Let me," Eulalia says. She's been sitting in one of the other chairs, off to the side like a spectator. She pushes herself up, walks to Frederick using all her femininity, throwing all her curves at him, including her smile. She's so incredibly beautiful, when she turns it on like that, her scars can't take away from it. "Frederick, dear," she says, leaning close and touching his forearm. "You want to save the world, do you not?"

Frederick trembles.

"You want to help us save the world, yes?" Her voice is smooth, soft, and sneaks under the skin.

Frederick averts his eyes, his whole head. "You have no power."

"None?" Eulalia pouts as she strokes the side of his face. It's as tender a motion as has ever been shared between two people. She turns his face toward hers. He meets her eyes. His lip quivers.

"Vermillion?" she prompts.

"Entirely mobilized."

"Against Jack?"

"Yes. No."

"No?"

He doesn't answer. He bites back his lips, closes his eyes. "You can't make me talk."

She whispers something to him, so softly even Jack, his senses all intensified over the last few days, cannot hear her. Frederick's eyes go wide, in disbelief or fear or something even more primal. His head drops, deflated and defeated. He says, "The fireplace."

"Which fireplace?" Eulalia asks. There's one on every floor, in the dining room, the master bedroom, the parlor, even the basement.

Tears spill, one at a time, from Frederick's eyes. He's shaking his head and sucking on his lips and attempting to sneer and scowl at the same time, making his face into a leathery mask of shadows and dark dances.

The fireplace in the basement is quite large, as are the others. It's encased in bricks with a precise, orderly array of implements. Firewood has been arranged inside, ready to burn. A quick search reveals a secret trigger that unlatches one of the bricks, and reveals a small cubbyhole empty of everything but a spider's web.

"It's a lie," Colton says.

Of course it is. Jack reaches in, through the web, and withdraws a black velvet pouch. Inside, he finds an ornate iron key, something someone spent a lot of time carving by hand, and a hobo nickel, a skull in profile on one side, a woman's face on the other. The key unlocks something important. The nickel hints at a history.

In his chair, Frederick laughs. It's vile. "Fate has you in its web, DarkWalker."

Jack holds up the key. "What does this open?"

"What do you think?"

"The apartment."

"Yes," Frederick says. Then: "No."

"You say that a lot."

"You'd be surprised how often it applies."

"He's playing games with the truth," Colton says. "It's not that he's resisting, but he's definitely fully aware of what he is and isn't saying."

"You're saying he's useless to us?"

"I don't know," Colton says. "What is it you want to accomplish now?"

Eulalia smiles. "Maybe we should rest?"

"The Brownstone is yours," Frederick says. "Do as you will."

"And you?"

"I serve the Order."

"I am the Order."

"We've been through this," Frederick says. "You're not the Order. You're just a Rogue. There's layers. You can't just come in and snap your fingers and watch all the bricks crumble like dominos. But I will tell you this, *DarkWalker*. You're not safe, you've never been safe and you never will be, not even when you're dead. You will hunt, and you will be hunted. Eventually, Fate will catch you." He snaps his fingers. "Crack you. Break you."

8.

Colton puts Frederick into a deep sleep. They leave him in his own apartment. By the time he wakes, they'll be gone, and he'll be free to do whatever he wants. Stay at the Brownstone, gather what remains of the Order, whatever.

They search the apartment again, especially the fireplaces, but find no apartment. Eventually, the three of them gather in the office. Jack takes the big desk. Eulalia takes the other. Lizzie's body remains in her bed, but Lance Turner is gone and the Brownstone is empty.

Standing over the globe, examining it, Colton asks, "When's the last time you slept, DarkWalker?"

Jack leans back in the chair. He feels exhaustion at the edges of his vision. "Eleven days? Twelve?"

"Perhaps," Colton says, "we should rest before what's next."

"What *is* next?" Eulalia asks.

Jack barely hesitates. "My father. He's still the architect behind this. He built the prison at Silver Blade. He sent me there. He assaulted me and Naomi, invaded our skin with tracking devices and poisons. He's – he's not my father anymore."

"Vengeance?" Colton asks.

"What else have I got?" No one answers that. How could they? "You're right. Sleep. It feels like a lifetime since I slept."

"Do you need something?" Colton asks.

"No."

"We should all sleep," Eulalia says. She's the first on her feet. "There are three unoccupied bedrooms upstairs."

Out the hall and up the stairs, Colton takes the second bedroom on the floor with Lizzie's corpse. Jack takes the South Room. The window there looks out at the back of a similar building on the next street. The bed is big and comfortable, but Jack sits on the edge for a long time. Like Frederick said, he doesn't feel safe. The man meant, of course, that Jack himself was the danger, but Jack feels very much under threat now. Jonathon Harlow is out there, at the head of Vermillion – the Tiger, as Diana Walcott put it. He'd arranged for Jack to be put into that prison. Why?

There's another DarkWalker at the bottom of that pit, an older DarkWalker, the first of their kind. Jack is only the sixth. The others are all dead or gone, which is difficult to explain and harder to comprehend. He doesn't linger on their fates. He doesn't linger on his own.

He lays down and closes his eyes when his head hits the pillow. He's tired, but not sleepy. There's a sound in the hallway, a soft footstep, someone approaching. He remains there, on top of the covers, eyes closed and unmoving as she turns the knob and pushes the door open. She thinks she's being stealthy, or at least quiet, and perhaps she is. She walks around the side of the bed, Jack's right side, her bare feet almost making no sound at all. She reaches for him.

Jack catches her wrist and opens his eyes. "You can't sneak up on me." He's looking up at Eulalia. She's wearing a robe she must have found in her room. She smiles. She does not, however, have her knife in hand, so he releases her.

"I can't sleep here," she says. "Not alone."

"I don't want..."

"It's not about what you want," Eulalia says. She

sheds the robe. Underneath, she's completely nude. The scars on her body are worse than the scars on her face, and some look fresh. "Move over."

She crawls into bed with him, alongside him, curled up against him, her body warm and her scent intoxicating.

"Do they hurt?" Jack asks. "The scars?"

She smiles sadly. "Yes."

Snuggled against him, she falls asleep. And perhaps the rhythm of her breathing lulls Jack Harlow into dreams.

9.

Jack Harlow dreams unpleasant dreams, but he sleeps, and he doesn't wake until Eulalia touches him, traces her fingers down his chest, kisses his throat. There's no passion between them, but there's urgency. The stronger she feels it, the stronger he feels it, and they find a rhythm not everyone can share. It's gentle, it's soothing, it eases her pain and his, even if only for a moment. When it's over, she remains snuggled against him and cries and says, "That was sweet," and she returns to sleep.

The unpleasant dreams persist, and this time Jack doesn't sleep long.

CHAPTER FIVE

JOHN URBANCIK

1.

Jack Harlow, DarkWalker, wakes at twilight. Through the window, the world is saturated with rich yellows and greens, even the bricks. Eulalia continues sleeping even after he climbs out of bed. He showers. It feels like weeks since he's seen a shower. He turns the hot faucet all the way and lets the water scald him. It doesn't hurt like it might have. The dirt and grime and dust and blood have insinuated into his skin, and it's a great effort to clean.

The nightmares don't stay with him, but they're definitely focused on those armies – the creatures he and Colton had seen in a vision, the legions Diana Walcott had claimed were amassed at the mountain. Under kings.

This may be the longest shower of his life. He scrubs, and lets the water just cascade over him, and breathes deeply of the steam as though it might clean him from the inside. His insides cannot be cleaned, but he might as well look and feel presentable. The odor he's been carrying, he knows, goes away, but the actual smell of him has changed. All sorts of things about him have changed.

When he emerges from the shadow, Eulalia is snoring softly.

Downstairs in the office, he finds Colton, also cleaned up, seated at the desk reading various papers and calendar books, flipping through a wood-paneled Rolodex filled with index cards. Colton looks up and shows Jack the card in his hand. "Typed," he says. "Some of these date back to the 1960s. Some seem relatively recent. A lot of updates made in pencil, to phone numbers mostly, and sometimes to names, especially for women who presumably married or un-married."

"Any names you recognize?" Jack asks.

"I've been under the earth for so long," Colton says, "you're lucky I recognize that these *are* names. No, I don't recognize any. Except one." It's the card in his hand. Jonathon Harlow. The original phone number had a 212 area code. It's scratched out in a faded pencil, but the second number is too faded to be legible. The third number, with a 516 area code, is the Long Island number Jack had grown up with.

Jack and Colton look at each other. Colton says, "I don't need to be a warlock to know there's a connection."

"Then let's make one," Jack says. He picks up the rotary phone – he's not sure he's ever used a rotary phone in his life – and dials each of the numbers, one at a time, taking the long way around the dial. Each number sounds like he's ripping through the phone circuits. "If it goes to the house," he says, "our house, where I grew up, I doubt there's anyone there to answer."

It connects halfway through the first ring. A tinny, distant woman's voice comes through. "You have reached the answering service for Jonathan Harlow. My name is Mercy. Would you like to leave a message?"

"Answering service?" Jack asks.

"Yes. My name is Mercy. I'll take your message and page Mr. Harlow with the details."

"How often does he respond to messages?"

"I couldn't rightly say, sir," Mercy tells him. "Who should I say is calling?"

"Jack Harlow."

Silence.

"Did you hear me?"

Mercy clears her throat. "Jack Harlow. Son. What message would you like to leave? And at what number can he return your call?" If not for the hesitation, Jack might think she's just an automated voice. But she's real. The pitch of her voice has gone up half an octave, and the words are just a little quicker. She's frightened.

"Tell him I'm at the Brownstone."

He waits for a response. Eventually, she says, "Please hold." There's a click, then music, uninspired jazz, as tinny and distant as the operator herself. Presumably, she's not merely *paging* Jonathan Harlow.

Another click, and Mercy says, "Mr. Harlow? Your father will see you soon."

"Thank you."

"He said to tell you he's disconnecting this number."

"I'm not sure I care."

"And he said he won't be alone."

"Neither will I."

There's a hesitation again before Mercy says, "May I ask you a personal question?"

"I might not answer it."

"Are you afraid?"

"Should I be?"

"I would be." There's another click, disconnecting the phone, followed by a fast busy signal. Jack puts the receive down.

"I guess we should expect company," Jack says.

The Brownstone is quiet for most the night. They go through files, finding all sorts of interesting trivialities, but nothing useful or necessary or helpful or applicable. A book detailing twenty-seven types of ghosts. The points of light on the globe appear to indicate the movement of something. Various collected trophies, artifacts, relics, and mementos line the shelves, some of which, according to Colton, the warlock, contain magical properties. Others might be just for show, or contains something other than magic. At least one appears to have a ghost attached to it, but the ghost is either not active or traveling.

Jack re-examines all the fireplaces, searching for something, anything, he might have missed. He looks at them, looks with senses he hasn't fully explored, searching for connections and threads and hints. He touches the ashes underneath the wood. He strokes the iron tools. He touches the bricks and listens to the bricks and tries to move each individual brick in each of the hearths. The brown and red bricks are mostly old, as old as the Brownstone, original to the building almost two hundred years ago, though some have been replaced and all of them have absorbed the sweat and blood and essence of the people who have lived here or slept under this roof. They're not all imbued with magic, not in the way some of the artifacts in the office are, but they have adapted to their environment.

And of course, Jack's sure he's missing things. There are threads he cannot see but can sense, knowledge he knows remains just outside of his reach. He's not all-powerful, not all-seeing, not all of anything. He's just a man. A man with extraordinary gifts, and curses, absorbed from everyone and everything he's been in contact with since birth.

Maybe he's going about it wrong. He's looking for a way through the fireplaces. Maybe he should be looking for a way to the Vermillion apartment. But changing his intentions, changing his methods, doesn't change the results.

At some point, Eulalia comes downstairs, showered, smelling of expensive perfume, wearing a black evening gown she found in a closet and an opal on a necklace. She searches through the library, perusing books but really searching for secrets – hidden keys or heirlooms, pages of family trees slipped in front of Bibles, handguns and cash, whatever else might be hidden within false books. Colton retreats to the kitchen at some point to conjure up a meal, and serves it in the dining room. It's nothing fancy, meat and vegetables and bread. Though they open what's presumably a good bottle of wine, Jack declines and the other two don't finish the bottle.

They are undisturbed throughout the night. No one knocks, the phone never rings, nobody uses a key to enter through the front, back, or basement. The rooftop terrace, perhaps the weakness strategic location in the Brownstone, is unaccosted. Colton says little, except during the meal, when he proclaims the spices he used and begs forgiveness for his lack of practice in the kitchen. "Once upon a time," he says, "I had the makings of a master chef."

Eulalia says almost nothing, but once or twice she throws demure smiles Jack's way.

Though the Brownstone's layout seems simple, with basically two suites on each floor except the ground level, the whole is actually bigger and difficult to navigate. The halls are straight, but the bedrooms hide additional rooms they didn't previously notice, closets and sitting rooms and private lounges, so many that the geography of the architecture defies physics. Jack finds a private office with a roll-top desk and two chairs and a shelf full of whiskey, scotch, and bourbon. He finds a woman's boudoir with a settee and filigreed furnishings and oil portraits on the wall. He finds a nursery, neat and unused, with old board games and wooden chess pieces.

There's a grandfather clock in the hall on the ground level, which is actually seven steps above the street. Throughout the day, it's remained silent, but it chimes when midnight strikes. The sound of it echoes throughout the halls, up and down the stairs and the elevator shaft, into the basement, behind the paintings and through the bookshelves, into workshops and priest holes that have thus far escaped Jack's notice, and into the apartment hiding within the walls, the apartment occupied by Vermillion, by surviving members of the Order of the White Raven, by Jonathan Harlow's lackeys and subordinates and servants and soldiers.

The apartment occupies another place as well, and now, with the striking of midnight echoing through the Brownstone, the doorways slide open. No, they're portals, connecting this Brownstone to another, and through the fireplaces on every floor, Vermillion arrives. They arrive in great numbers. They arrive armed, locked and loaded, cocked and ready to shoot. They carry weapons other than guns, but they also carry guns. They carry knives and poisons and tinctures of various sorts, and among them there's a warlock younger and more vibrant than Colton, there's a vampire, there's a ghost, and there's their leader – the head of the tiger – no, the *spider* – Jack's father, Jonathan Harlow.

2.

"The things you've made me do," Jonathan Harlow says, stepping straight up to his son.

"I'm not who I was."

"You never were." Jonathan motions with his fingers, and someone steps forward with a variation of a Taser. The electricity leaps through Jack's nerve endings and muscles, and red briefly overrides his senses.

3.

He's only out of it briefly. He wakes with his hands cuffed in front of him and restraints tying him down to the billiards table in the basement. The light is dimmer than he remembers. He doesn't immediately open his eyes, just his other senses. He hears movement throughout the Brownstone and voices crackling over walkie-talkies. "Parlor is secure." "We've got his friend." "She doesn't match known associates." "What do you mean, human?" "Check the Silver Blade files, you'll find her."

He counts the footsteps of three individual people in the basement with him, but the breathing patterns of at least four others. Someone's typing on a keyboard. Someone's sitting on the throne.

"I tried to keep you out of it," Jonathan Harlow says.

Jack opens his eyes. The binds hold down his neck, as well, so he can only barely, in periphery, see his father on the big chair.

"I tried to make you realize the organization was flawed," Jonathan says, "and I gave you the house."

"I didn't want a house."

"If the Council had realized the threat you posed," Jonathan says, "they would have had you exterminated in Orlando."

Jack rattles the chains. "*I'm* the threat?"

Lance Turner's voice adds, "He could've taken the Susquehanna Facility by himself, but he subverted agents of darkness to his cause." Jack can't see Lance, but he's somewhere near the stairs. His voice quivers as it's never done before. "He murdered your daughter. My wife. The mother of my child."

Jack tests the strength of the iron holding him. No, not iron, it's carbon fiber with iron and silver and garlic and seven distinct venoms shot through it. They're designed to hold a variety of creatures, and might be effective against many. But Jack Harlow, DarkWalker, is a composite of many creatures, and his strengths aren't purely any one of them. He doesn't have their weaknesses. He won't be surprised again. "I didn't mean to kill her," Jack says.

"I know." Jonathan's voice – his father's voice – is tinged with sorrow and regret and the same coldness that's always underlined it. "But you *did* kill her."

Jack feels compelled to defend himself. "She shot me."

"That doesn't matter anymore," Jonathan says. "What matters is, your power has grown exponentially since I last saw you. It wasn't even that long ago."

Someone hands Jonathan a tablet, diverting his attention. Lance, however, remains close, and Jack sees him now, trying to keep his distance but unable to disguise his disgust. "You know I didn't mean to do it."

"It's not about intention," Lance tells him. "In fact, it's about your lack of intention. You're uncontrolled, Jack Harlow. You're unstable. You're a monster."

"What happened to Colton and Eulalia?"

Lance smiles. Jack hears the sound of it even if he can't quite see it from this angle. "Colton has been retained. Eulalia..." He shakes his head. "She resisted."

"What happened?"

"Shot. Seven times." Lance's smile drops. "They assumed she was something more than human."

"And you call me monster."

"You brought her into this."

"Doesn't matter," Jonathan says, interrupting. "There are three active threats right now, and this one – my so-called *son* – is the lowest priority." He comes down from the throne and approaches the billiards table. "Jack, if I have these binds removed, will you behave yourself?"

Jack shakes his head, though it's a restricted movement. "Assume I'm unstable and unreliable."

"Oh, I do." Jonathan leans over him. "But I raised you as my own, Jack, and even still I feel compelled to protect you."

"Sir." Lance, but he's ignored.

"If you had stayed on Long Island, you wouldn't have become an issue."

"Stayed when you gave me the house? Or stayed after mom died?"

Jonathan shakes his head. "You can't undo your mistakes, Jack."

"And what do you mean, *as* your own?"

Jonathan ignores the question. "I'm going to make you an offer. The same offer I made previously, really. I want you to join. Enlist. Pledge yourself to our cause."

"Your cause?"

"I told you before, the organization – the White Ravens – didn't do anything. They weren't really supposed to, I know, I stretched the truth a little, they were just meant to gather and analyze intel. But the Tiger was formed almost two thousand years ago to combat those threats. You're no longer a watcher, or primarily a watcher, so you can stand against the darkness. There's still a chance to save you, to save your soul, and, Jack, to save the world."

Jack Harlow closes his eyes again. "Release me."

"Will you help us?"

"Release me," Jack says again.

"I need assurances, Jack."

"That," Jack says, "is the last time I ask for anything twice."

A stillness fills the basement. Everyone within earshot senses the threat, even if it's just the undercurrent beneath Jack's intentions. They see his curled fists, can probably see the blood angrily pumping through the veins at his neck. Redder blood than theirs. When no one moves, when no one attempts to unlock the cuffs or untie the restraints, Jack Harlow does it himself. Since meeting Nick Hunter, then a vampire hunter, Jack's been able to coax the internal mechanisms of all sorts of locks. Since his time under the mine at Silver Blade, he's got strength enough to shatter them. He's absorbed other abilities, mostly untested. He doesn't know what he can or cannot do. He focuses on all the things tying him down, the irons and alloys and venoms and everything. He focuses on the anger inside him, boiling and seething and corrosive, and draws from it. The cuffs, the tethers and chains, melt. Even as he sits up, the billiards table itself succumbs, more than he'd intended. The felt top shimmers like liquid mercury.

Guards, four of them, react instantly, with weapons that had never been holstered. The guns and blades also melt, even without Jack's direct attention. One of the guards screams as his hand, too, liquefies.

Lance Turner, coward, retreats until his back hits the wall.

Jonathan Harlow, however, stands his ground.

Jack descends from the billiards table. He walks straight up to his father. The old man is taller than him, by two or three inches, and his hair is peppered with white. Otherwise, they really look nothing alike. Jack's eyes, his bone structure, all that came from his mother. Looking up at his father now, his so-called father, he no longer feels cowed or compliant or fearful. He no longer feels disdain for the absence, all the cards and letters from distant corners of the earth. He feels only anger.

"All I wanted," Jack says, "was to be left alone. You couldn't do that, could you? You had to send – you sent everything, didn't you? The handler, the seer in the mines, even the other DarkWalker."

Ah, but you don't always need words to betray secrets. When Jack says *DarkWalker*, his father's pupils dilate. His breathing pattern is disrupted. It's all very underneath, well concealed, and no one else would see it.

"If I *am* a threat," Jack Harlow says, "I'm the threat you designed."

Jonathan Harlow shakes his head. "Not a threat to me, or to Vermillion, but to the world. We don't care about the individuals. We don't care if a vampire drinks or fucks or kills every night of its limited eternity. But when something threatens to destroy everything, when something like the Prince of Thorns is allowed to return to the earth again, that requires action. You allowed that, you facilitated that, you made that happen, and that had nothing to do with us." Jonathan takes a breath. "Hell, the Thorns is why the Prince of the Stable Door established the Tiger. To defend the realm."

"I put down the Prince of Thorns."

"You told the kings, all of them, that the earth was a place they could reach again, Jack. You broke the barriers, you shattered protections as old as humanity. And now I'm asking, Jack, I'm asking for you to help us contain what you've unleased."

Jack restrains his anger. He could reach into Jonathan's chest and rip the heart out through the ribs. He could shatter every bone in the old man's body. He could melt Jonathan Harlow's brain inside his skull until it drips out his tear ducts and nostrils and ears and pores. "I have questions."

Jonathan nods with his eyes.

"What did you do with Eulalia?"

"She was shot," Jonathan admits. "There's a nurse with her now. She'll probably survive."

"Shot seven times?"

"Give or take."

"Why isn't she dead?"

"You might answer that one," Jonathan says. The scars, of course, the lifetimes she's accumulated. Jack doesn't know how those work.

"What happened to Naomi?"

Jonathan shakes his head. "That's one question we've been unable to answer."

"What happened to Nick Hunter?"

"I'd assumed he died under the mine."

"You know that's not true."

Jonathan glances at Lance. "I know it *now*. The last report saw him in Richmond, Virginia. He's a vampire now."

"You did that."

"That's not a question."

"What happened to mom?"

A beat. The briefest hesitation, a moment of grief breaking through Jonathan Harlow's mask, a moment shared between the two of them, the husband and the son. "She died."

"That's not enough."

"We can talk about it later," Jonathan says. He glances at the fireplace. "You have the key?"

"Yes."

"I need you to go to Shangri La," Jonathan says, "and put down the kings and their armies."

"Shangri La?"

"In the valley of the mountain Armageddon."

4.

The soldier with the melted hand is taken away. The others stay clear of the billiards table, its surface shimmering like a dark lake. Lance Turner stands against the wall, the stone mask of his face cracked by his lips, a straight slash yet somehow scowling, frowning, and angry all at the same time. Jonathan Harlow stands like a king, like an emperor, wanting to send his minions to take care of some minor scuffle in the mountains. Jack Harlow stares at his father, his so-called father, and remembers things buried, forgotten, and lost.

Jonathan Harlow returning from a work trip to Eastern Europe, where he'd been ambushed by former Soviet spies. "They have their own unit," he'd said when he didn't think Jack or Lizzie were near.

Jonathan Harlow bringing gifts of dice from Turkey. "These are just dice," his father said, "but there, in the Anatolian fields, there was once a man who carved dice from the skulls of his enemies."

Jonathan Harlow making waffles with scoops of vanilla ice cream on top for Jack and Lizzie. "It's the only proper way, you understand."

Jonathan Harlow at Jack's mom's funeral, standing in the sunlight, dressed in black and sweating like everyone else, a solid, unspeaking wall.

Jonathan Harlow holding a microchip. "Once this is inside you, we can track you by satellite anywhere in this world, and we can, should our little organization be put in jeopardy, we can and will release its poison in your bloodstream. Don't worry, though, if it comes to that, son, it'll be a painless death."

There are contradictions. The father. The victim. The man so devoted to his work he often forgot he had family or a home. The lying, manipulative figurehead at the front of Vermillion trying to convince Jack Harlow to risk his life.

"I should just forgive everything?" Jack asks.

"It's all past us now, son."

"You don't mean that. *Son*. Who am I, really?"

Jonathan Harlow smiles. There's not an ounce of true feeling there. "I raised you."

"Is that what you call it?"

"You bear my name."

"My mother's name."

Jonathan shakes his head. "Not my truth to tell. Ask your mother."

Jack punches his father in the face.

It comes out of nowhere. Jack doesn't think about it, just reacts. The fist is flying before he even knows it is, and he knows he's got strength enough to shatter bones. He pulls back at the last minute, stops it from being fatal, but it throws Jonathan back and down. It draws blood. A trickle from the lips. Jonathan's nose is busted and crooked. And it feels damn good. Jack stands over this man who has pretended to be his father for so long, fists clenched, and says, "I should kill you."

Jonathan wipes blood from his face with the back of his hand. "You should."

"Give me a reason, a good reason, not to." Jack's fists are clenched so tight, the basement lights – all the lights of the Brownstone, maybe all of West 35th Street, maybe the entire island of Manhattan – flicker.

Lance Turner moves, presumably to hold Jack back, to stop him somehow. Or hurt him. Whatever Lance's intentions, Jack catches him by the throat. Squeezes. He feels the brittle bones, the windpipe, the esophagus, the vertebrae in Lance's neck twisting under his fist.

That's when the vampire and ghost move in.

Just as Jack's releasing Lance, all red-faced and breathless, the vampire tackles him from behind. He's a strong vampire, powerful and perhaps a thousand years old, with skin like alabaster and teeth like a shark. They go down together. Jack catches the vampire's arms by the wrists, both of them, and with his teeth tears into the vampire's throat. Not to drink. To rip and tear and shred. His teeth aren't the elongated canines of the predator, but Jack's human physiology allows him to do some damage.

The vampire tries to get away, but Jack holds him tight, and Jack spits a chunk of flesh into the vampire's face.

The ghost grabs him.

Ghosts are rarely corporeal. Ghosts rarely interact with the material world because they're not strong enough, or concentrated enough, or emotional enough. This ghost, insubstantial and impossible to grab, nevertheless carries the weight of the Brownstone, and crushes Jack through the rug to the concrete floor, threatens to drop them into another basement below. But Jack's seen too many ghosts to count. He manages to get his fingers around the ghost's insubstantial throat as though it's flesh. The ghost is surprised. Shocked. The ghost tries to pull away. Jack reaches into its chest and rips it apart.

Ghost innards splatter the basement and everyone in it. Those who remain, the few soldiers, the wounded vampire, Lance, even Jonathan Harlow, stare. Calmly, without any display of bravado, Jack picks himself up and, standing, takes command of the basement. He looks down at his father. "I'm still waiting for that reason."

Coughing, struggling to catch his breath, Lance says, "I can give you a reason."

Jack looks at him. "I can't trust you anymore."

"You never really did."

"Then I actively *distrust* you."

"Those armies," Lance says. "Seven kings, seven armies, on the mountain of Armageddon. They're gathering now, and when they're ready, they'll descend on the earth."

"Not my fault. No matter what he says."

"Maybe it was inevitable," Jonathan says, standing. "Maybe those armies were always going to gather. But they're coming through now because they think the world is weak. Because they believe they have destroyed the Tiger."

"The Mystic Ninja," Jack says. "And the Prince of the Stable Door."

"Vermillion is just one leg of the Tiger," Jonathan says. "One leg of the spider. Just as the White Ravens was only one aspect of the watchers."

"You sent the mystic ninja?"

"They never answered to me," Jonathan says. "But I know what they did. What you did on Long Island. *At home.*"

"I assume you have an army," Jack says.

Jonathan nods.

"I want complete control. I say jump, they jump. I say die, they don't bother asking how, they just kill themselves in the most expedient way."

"My soldiers are yours," Jonathan says.

"And where do you plan to hide?" Jack asks.

"I'll be gathering more of our allies."

Jack shakes his head. "No. Not good enough. Lance can do that instead. You're coming with me to the mountain." Jack holds up the ornate iron key he'd found in the fireplace cubbyhole. "And when it's over, if you're still alive, you and I are going to have words."

JOHN URBANCIK

PART TWO
ARMAGEDDON

JOHN URBANCIK

CHAPTER ONE

JOHN URBANCIK

1.

In the office, Jonathan Harlow has one of his men tell Jack what they know.

2.

In the long ago, before time was counted in a way we understand, a series of battles raged over the fate of the earth. Some were won, some were lost, some were fought to a draw. Gods and entities and powers and concepts warred for the greatest of prizes. A great many heroes were lost on both sides. This was before humans or ghosts or vampires or werewolves. All of that came later. This was a time of angels and demons and djinn and celestials and infernals and demigods and heroes. From this place, all our myths were born, and from this place, all our nightmares have their roots.

There were kings and princes, queens and princesses, and ultimately, all any of them succeeded in doing was fracturing the nature of reality and condemning their enemies to certain realms.

"You have to understand," Jonathan Harlow's man says, "We have no real records of these times, only stories, and only stories passed down from survivor to survivor, and there's no real reason to believe any of this."

The children of these beings and powers eventually gave us the creatures of the dark and the light, beasts and saviors alike. But these offspring continued to fight, continued to deny each other whatever they could. The one thing they all had in common, apparently, was a desire to be the last standing.

"We've no record of their names," Jonathan Harlow's man says. "They're not just forgotten, they were lost before there was a such thing as history."

When the human race came into existence, they slowly, and with great difficulty, took over. They dominated the planet. They drove back the powers, they defeated the darkness, and they conquered the light. They propagated. Humans were inherently creatures of the land, taking the fields and the forests, the meadows and the mountains, the plateaus and plains and deserts and tundra. They dug into caves and caverns and mines and pits. Then they took to the seas, and overcame a great many ancient powers, krakens and leviathans and squid and elder creatures from the depths of space. Eventually, they even took to the skies, first by commandeering creatures of flight, they devastating those creatures with their own flying machines.

They even reached beyond the earth's surface, into the endless of abyss of space.

Sometimes, though, something would break through from other realms, like the Prince of Thorns, who shattered three dimensions of hell to reach the walled city Jack Harlow had, himself, destroyed.

"Personally," Jonathan Harlow's man confides, "I don't blame you for that. I've read your file. I know what you were seeking – who you were seeking – I just think you went about it wrong."

The Prince of Thorns had previously been put down by the Prince of the Stable Door. The names, of course, were poor translations. The mystic ninja were originally the Order of the Tiger, and their martial styles still influence many of today's fighting arts. The Spider – yes, Vermillion was never a Tiger, but a red spider with a black mark – the Spider put down an uprising of hellions in Germany's Black Forest, and the Spider prevented a portal from opening in the waters of Casablanca, and the Spider destroyed a talisman that might've ripped open an Olmec pyramid in Mexico.

But Vermillion was only able to accomplish these things because they had recruited some powerful creatures – vampires, ogres, ghosts, pythons and vipers, even a minotaur – and because they were mostly preventative.

But after the Prince of Thorns found his way through, other ancient kings followed, on the order of demons and demigods. And the Seven, as they were always known, whose wars decimated deserts and leveled forests and cracked the very earth, have risen through known portals and punched their way through weaknesses in the fabric of reality and brought with them their armies and a new, deeper kind of darkness that will swallow the earth.

Jonathan Harlow's man says, "It's some apocalyptic shit, let me tell you."

Jack asks, "Do we know anything about them?"

"Specifics?" Jonathan Harlow's man shakes his head. "Not even their names."

"Why are they gathering at Armageddon?"

"Prophecy? Convenience?"

"What are they waiting for? Why haven't they attacked already?"

"They have."

Jonathan Harlow adds, "The region has lost seven settlements. Not huge numbers, hundreds perhaps in each, but that's just in the past twenty-four hours. Since we've been dealing with you, and the Susquehanna Incident, and the damn DarkCrawler."

"I don't know what that is."

"One of our own," Jonathan Harlow says. "The point is, we need someone capable of fighting, and you're it. We saw what you did to our vampire. To our ghost. No one's been able to touch a ghost before. You fought the Prince of Thorns and defeated him."

"I wasn't quite myself then," Jack admits.

"But you retained *all of it,*" Jonathan says. "This is a battle you have to fight. It's just a question of will you fight it now, on your own terms, or when they've taken the earth and they've got you surrounded and there's no place left to hide."

"How many men do we have?"

"One hundred soldiers. One vampire. One minotaur. One python." Jonathan Harlow frowns. " We had a ghost."

"That doesn't seem like much of an army," Jack admits.

"We'll be supporting a force already at Shangri La."

"All at my command, then?" Jack asks.

"Yes."

"And the warlock?"

"Your friend," Jonathan Harlow says, "is currently detained."

"Let me talk to him."

3.

"Do you trust them?" Colton asks. They're sitting across from each other at an antique table in one of the parlors. Jack's not sure if the room is actually in Manhattan anymore, but the connection is visible – at least to him.

"No," Jack says. "But I do believe them."

"Our vision, then," Colton says. "We probably saw one of these armies."

"There are seven," Jack says.

"I suspect it wasn't merely a vision," Colton says. "It had the feel of a prophecy to it."

To his knowledge, Jack's never known a prognosticator, not one with real skill, though he may have picked up a trace of the ability from something behind a wall in Silver Blade, or from something in one of the many hells he's visited, or even just in his travels. He's been wrong about the nature of creatures before, because he was never truly a watcher and the distance had allowed the power to wane by the time he reached Orlando. Now, everything inside him churns. Jack points out, "It was just an image. An army in darkness."

"Shared by you and I," Colton says. "That's important. It means I don't have a choice. I'm going with you. And this is how I die."

"What?"

"I've had a vision myself, once," Colton says. "It was a side-effect of a powerful spell I cast, I want to say on Coney Island, when I was just a kid." He takes a breath. "I didn't get what I was wanting that day. I didn't know everything I needed to know about carousels that day."

"Someday," Jack says, "it might be interesting to know the things you've seen and done."

Colton shakes his head. "It won't happen. Tomorrow is the day I die. Better to do it on a battlefield than in a Brownstone."

"We're going to need some powerful work," Jack says.

"I have a few powerful invocations," Colton admits. "I always feared I'd die in that damned mine."

"Did you do something," Jack says, "that convinced them you needed to be imprisoned."

Colton grins. "I can think of a thing or two." But he doesn't elaborate, and Jack doesn't press it.

Jack stands. "I want to see Eulalia."

4.

They have Eulalia in Lizzie's bed Lizzie. The corpse is gone. Tubes connect an IV to Eulalia, and there's monitoring equipment, and a nurse named Geoff. When Jack enters the room, Geoff looks up from a chart and says, "She should be dead. Very fucking dead. Dead a hundred times over, dead."

"She's not," Jack says.

"I'm a watcher," Geoff says. "I know what a thing is when I see it. She's more human than you or me."

Eulalia's scars are all in flames, running red as though they're fresh and bleeding. They're bizarrely captivating. The scars crisscross her body at random but take on abstract meanings if you spend too much time looking at them.

"You have her file?" Jack asks.

Geoff nods.

"Who sent her into Silver Blade?"

"Ain't got that," Geoff says. "There's no file on her before today. We wouldn't even know her fucking name if not for you. Like I said. Human. Why the fuck would we care?"

Jack knows the answer to that. He also know the nurse isn't lying.

"You wanted to see her, now you've seen her," Geoff says. "Better leave the care to the fucking caregivers."

Jack gives him a look that might've withered other men. Geoff stands his ground, but makes no move the remove him, so Jack steps forward and takes Eulalia's hand. He's got healing skills of some sort, positive energies, revivification abilities, but he doesn't really know how to use them. He saved Colton earlier, but could do nothing for his sister. Jack closes his eyes. He's tired of death.

Eulalia's eyes flicker. She moves her lips. Jack leans closer to hear, but she's not making a sound. Instead, her words seep into his skin through her fingers.

"What's she saying?" Geoff asks.

Jack releases her hand, turns to go, but pauses at the door. *"Just another scar."*

5.

The soldiers gather. Vampire. Minotaur. Python. Warlock. Jonathan Harlow, Spider, in his made to order black suit and red, red tie. And Jack Harlow, DarkWalker, with the key in hand.

The portal is on the rooftop terrace. It's fancy up here, with low couches and lights and marble statues and wet bars on both sides, views between the Manhattan canyons in two directions. The eastern sky shows signs of the impending sunrise, a thin line of red against the horizon.

Two columns, supporting a trellis roof, combine to form a kind of portal. Hidden earlier, missed by Jack and Colton, is the keyhole. The iron key in Jack's hands warms as he approaches. He couldn't have opened this lock on his own; it's not merely a series of mechanisms, but part of a kind of spellwork.

"It's a long time, since I was last in Shangri La," Jonathan Harlow says.

Jack doesn't acknowledge it. But he realizes he's in his father's territory, still subject to rules he doesn't care to understand, and he cannot forget the threat at his back. They've acknowledged three threats, and Jack is one of them. He can't pretend they've forgotten this.

He inserts the key. A warmth flows through his arm as he turns it. The mechanisms respond, the spell is enacted, and the environment shifts. Through the columns, there's another land, another world, higher in humidity and richer in color, with different textures and odors. The soldiers go through at double time. Jack, Colton, and Jonathan Harlow step through together.

The cityscape of New York is replaced by Shangri La.

They arrive on a rooftop terrace not dissimilar from where they left, but the city of Shangri La is organic, the color of mountains and forests, its tallest spires nothing as high as the skyscrapers of New York but no less impressive. Narrow bridges connect bits of the city with the side of the mountain. A river flows through the city, fed by waterfalls from the closest mountain. They're in a valley among mountains capped by snow and ice, but here it's warm and thick and overgrown.

There's birds, and a herd of something like antelope leaping through the city streets, all in a singular direction.

Jack looks where they're running from.

On this side of the world, it's sunset, and the clouds of the western sky drip with fire and blood. In the east, in the darkness, enshrouded in its own clouds, is the mountain Armageddon. Whereas the other mountains blend seamlessly into the scene, and in fact create the scene, Armageddon stands alone and lifeless, without a tree, without streams and waterfalls, seemingly without life of any sort. Scorched and ashen, craggy, jagged, and cracked, the mountain looms like a nightmare. Smoke rises from vents as though it's a volcano. It vibrates with the movement of armies within its bowels. Arcs of unnatural lightning flash through the smoke and clouds around it. Eyes inside, on the face of the mountain, at the summit, witness the arrival of Jack Harlow and his little army.

"Why would you build Shangri La in the shadow of that?" Jack asks.

"Paradise," Jonathan Harlow says, "stands in opposition to damnation."

There are people in the streets of Shangri La, and in the houses, staring at terrace. They're on top of a temple at the end of the world. The soldiers are already descending into the building.

"Come," Jonathan says, gesturing toward a particular doorway. "We're expected."

6.

They meet Kalinda in the main hall of the temple. Her skin's dark, her accent purely Australian, and her eyes make Jack – would make any person – uncomfortable. She looks into souls. She's a seer, in the way Tania, in the mines of Silver Blade, was a seer, not seeing futures yet seeing well beyond what's obvious.

She's there with four soldiers of her own. She looks at Jack Harlow, spends all of the first minute looking at and examining the DarkWalker, then says to Jonathan, "We have kept the city, but they've circled around us and tunneled under us and I'm afraid they'll be going over us next." She looks at Jack again. "They attack at *ukamirra.*"

Jonathan looks to the east though they're indoors. "Will they come here?"

"They will."

"Then we'll defend the city again tonight."

"We'll defend *this* city," Kalinda says, "but watch another one fall. Again." She returns her attention to the DarkWalker. "What do you see, when you look at me, DarkWalker?"

Jack smiles. It's not filled with humor. "I see age."

"I'm old, yes."

"And beauty."

"I have maintained the evil beauty of youth." She walks around him. Circles him like a shark. She's not like Jonathan Harlow at all. In control but not because of fear, not because of manipulation, but because of wisdom and experience and respect.

"You've fought before."

"All of us have."

"You've fought here before. Against the forces of darkness."

"Every day, love."

Jack frowns. He concentrates. "You've kept the terrors of Armageddon within the mountain for a thousand years." He corrects himself. "Not you, personally, but your ancestors. Every generation, you face a test."

"This is my test," Kalinda says. "Tell me more."

"Shangri La isn't on any map," Jack say, "because we're not, strictly speaking, on earth."

"We are *of* the earth," Kalinda says.

"The portal we used to get here, it's not the only one."

"Love, *all* of Shangri La is a portal."

"But there are other cities here."

"The eleven paradises, yes."

Jack's confused. "Do they all stand against darkness?"

"We all stand against the same darkness."

Jack looks at Jonathan Harlow. "And this darkness, these armies, these *kings*, are not here because of anything I've done. They're always here."

"They're not always active," Jonathan Harlow says.

Kalinda holds up a hand to shush him. "This is between you and I, DarkWalker."

"What do you know about me?"

She shakes her head. "We can discuss that another time. Do you feel the rumble of the mountain?"

Indeed, he does. The vibrations reach through the earth, causing the leaves to tremble in the trees, sending even the predators running in search of safer ground.

"We are of the Tiger here," Kalinda says. "And *we* have never lost our way." She spares a glance at

Jonathan Harlow but touches Jack's arm. "You, however, are unique. Because there are stories of DarkWalkers past, but only stories, only whispers. There has never been one on this side of the mountain."

Jack tilts his head. The temple has a great many tall windows. The mountain outside of Shangri La reminds him of undreamt nightmares. "Do you know of a DarkWalker inside the mountain?"

"Once upon a time, love," Kalinda says, "but history is long and there's no longer any such thing. Except for you."

"Actually," Jonathan Harlow says, "we have reason to believe there's at least one other."

"Your *DarkCrawler*?" Kalinda practically spits the word. "You allowed that thing to manifest within your very walls. You nurtured it until it turned against you."

"We didn't know."

"Blindness," Kalinda says, "is the first defense of ignorance."

The trembling in the earth grows more intense. It's the vibrations of seven legions of feet pounding the earth and advancing upon the city.

"Let's see what you can do," Kalinda says, leading Jack toward the main doors of the temple. "Can you stop them?"

"Me alone?"

"Impress me, love. And impress the kings."

The city of Shangri La has no definitive border. It exists as part of the mountain forest, so there's no demarcation, but Kalinda leads them to a particular spot along a wall that looks like it grew out from the earth intact. They stand with red skies behind them so that their shadows point at the mountain.

"Do you feel them?" Kalinda asks Jack.

He does. As the army comes closer, he feels their footsteps through his own feet. But he also feels their pain, their anguish, their anger. It touches his own, so he clenches his fists and his teeth.

"Do you hear their individual heartbeats?" Kalinda asks. "Do you see their dreams and their hopes?"

"I see...something."

Kalinda squeezes his hand. It's as though everyone else has faded away and time has stopped, though the rumbling grows ever more persistent. "You're beginning to see that the creatures of the night are not just the monsters we assume."

"Why are you showing me this?" Jack asks. "I thought we were supposed to be defending the world."

"The world," Kalinda says, "is broader than you think."

"And the army?"

"Fodder," Kalinda says. "Slaves. Distractions."

"The true threat is the kings."

Kalinda smiles. "Yes. But that doesn't mean their armies are not a threat."

And the legion arrives.

One king's army, with one king at the back whipping up their fervor, shouting orders, sending his monsters to fight and die. The creatures arrive in formation, armed with swords and bludgeons and spears and rifles as well as their claws and teeth and venoms and acids. There are a thousand of them, each different from every other, each creature the only of its kind, beasts with names Jack Harlow cannot decipher or comprehend. There are too many of them, and the languages too old, with names never meant for human tongues.

The soldiers on Jack's side of the war had already set up a perimeter. They never waited for Jack's orders. He was never really going to be their general, and that's okay. He knows nothing of military strategy. Jonathan Harlow is issuing commands. The vampire, the minotaur, and the python have already been deployed – where to, Jack doesn't know, though he can reach out and sense them along the lines if he tries. The warlock, Colton, stands beside him, the warlock who knows he dies tomorrow, and the reality of everything reaches Jack. His heart breaks for all the loss, all the suffering, that's about to happen.

"I don't want to do this," Jack tells Kalinda.

She smiles, squeezes his hand one last time before releasing it, and says, "Neither do I. But we must."

The battle starts somewhere to the north, where another phalanx of the same army rushes forth from the trees. There's gunfire and explosions and smoke and screaming, first the kind meant to instill terror, the scream of warriors running into battle knowing it's likely to be their last. On both sides.

The creatures in the army, some of them, seem recognizable, borrowing shapes from actual animals, crocodiles and falcons and wildebeests and the like. Others are nearly indescribable, amorphous, more akin to rocks or clouds or glass.

Kalinda says, "Ready?"

She doesn't wait for an answer. She rushes forward, toward the advancing army, toward the overwhelming numbers, brandishing a spear of some sort Jack's never seen. He runs after her, not knowing what else to do, with only his closed fists and the energy contained within them.

His first punch catches one of the rocklike beasts in the center of its head. It didn't recognize Jack as a threat. It did nothing to defend itself. It cracks in half, right down the middle, with a concussive force that shakes the earth. Around him, briefly, the other enemy soldiers stare in awe at their new target. And they converge, all of them, as though the entire army exists with only one purpose.

Behind the lines, Colton casts spells that give Jack strength. He feels the surges of that energy. But Jack's also absorbing the powers and aptitudes of every demonic beast near him. When one strikes him from behind, its claws rake his back as though Jack's made of rock, and the force of the blow doubles back and shatters the bony ridges in the creature's arm, shoulder, and back. It practically explodes with the impact.

Jack Harlow has never felt stronger or more frightened. He doesn't know what can touch him, if anything can touch him. He's sure he can die. He almost died just yesterday of a gunshot wound. But now, he's shifting between the abilities of creatures he's never imagined. He's partly invisible one moment, gelatinous the next, then acidic, then granite. He crushes his opposition, shattering bones and sundering flesh. He blinds the creatures, and sears the creatures, and ploughs through them.

He doesn't know if it's a long battle. He doesn't know how much blood he's spilt. On the battlefield, he sees Kalinda beside him. She's defending him now, fighting back the creatures that have only eyes for him. The city is no longer under siege. They want the DarkWalker.

The king shouts his orders and throws his own thunderbolts, which explode on the battlefield and incinerate soldiers from both sides. Even the king's weapons can't seem to touch Jack, but they're being deflected by the efforts of others.

Some of the blood on Jack's fists is his own. He's not invulnerable.

A hydra of sorts, part electric eel and part elephant, bears down on him with a dozen barbed trunks. It smashes Jack with its spikes from both sides and spills venoms into Jack's bloodstream. The creature screams triumphantly, and raises its front legs to crush Jack beneath them. There's no one to protect him, so Jack attempts to catch the feet, to stop the creature. But he's not that strong. It buries him in the dirt. It crushes his breath. It steals his vision and his heartbeat, even if only for a moment.

Every war has its fallen soldiers. Some wars have heroes. Those heroes are not always the soldiers, and not always known to the rest of the world. Sometimes, they are only heroes to one person. But to that one person, they are everything. Jack Harlow, DarkWalker, is no hero, not to anyone on this field or any other, but he's fought beside heroes.

Kalinda is a hero. She beats back the elephantine eel hydra with her spear, blinding both eyes and hobbling its back legs and slicing three tentacles clean off. Jack, under the bulk of it for a moment, is wounded, his ribs crushed, his legs shattered, and his vision blurred. He feels pain from inside and out.

Colton kneels beside him, enacting some sort of pre-planned spellwork, something to lessen the pain and reverse the worst of the damage. The warlock is a hero. The warlock is a hero who will die for his cause.

Jonathan Harlow, somewhere behind the lines, is no hero.

Jack struggles to see moonlight, to see the stars, to know which direction is Shanri La and which direction is Armageddon, but it's all struggle. He's broken, inside, in ways he didn't think a person should live through.

CHAPTER TWO

1.

Jack Harlow descends into dreams. Nightmares.

It's a nightscape he barely recognizes, one of the hells he witnessed in his travels, one where he didn't stay. A dozen or more had flashed by him. He's there now, sitting on the edge of a narrow bridge, talking with himself, and other versions of himself, a dozen or more gathered there.

He's not sure which he is.

He says, "What did you expect would happen?"

"You're not a warrior, Jack."

"You're not a fighter."

"A little bit of an inheritance, and suddenly you think you're some sort of god?"

All the Jack Harlows laugh.

"You're not a savior or a hero or a warrior of any sort," he says.

"What am I, then?"

The Jacks laugh again. "Isn't it obvious?"

"You're angry."

"You're furious."

"With your daddy."

"Jonathan Harlow?"

More laughter. "An imposter. A fake. A false idol."

"Burn the heretic," one of the flying Jacks says. Jack didn't even realize there were Jacks in the air, but there they are, above and below the bridge, on wings or simply floating, or hanging from a thread connected to something he cannot see. He knows it's not real. He feels pain in the dust of his bones, and there shouldn't be any dust.

"Then who?" Jack asks. "Who am I mad at?"

"Who ain't you mad at?"

"You're mad at me," Lance says, though he appears only briefly.

"You're mad at me," Lizzie says. "How'd that go?"

"And me," Rowan says, his sister's daughter, his niece, whom he's never seen and didn't know existed.

"And me," Tania says, the seer from the mine.

"You're downright furious with me," Jonathan Harlow says, "but you can't bring yourself to take care of me, can you?"

"I'm not a murderer," Jack says.

The guard from the shack at the Susquehanna Facility says, "No?"

"You're mad at me," one of the Jacks says.

"And me," another says.

"You're especially mad at me," a third says.

Jack says, "Stop."

"You're even mad at me." And for a moment, the rest of the world, this dream world, disappears, and all that's there is Lisa Sparrow. She's close, but she's not really there, there's nothing of her in the image – only a reflection of himself. "I didn't want to leave you," she says.

"You should be mad at me," the demon says, the red-skinned demon who had tortured Lisa Sparrow.

"Even me." Jia Li, the vampire who had abducted him in Orlando, who had then proceeded to fight to protect him.

"But there's no reason to be mad with me," Kalinda says, stepping through the mist and dispelling the others. She walks right up to him, kneels so she can look Jack in the eyes, and says, "All I did was lead you into a battle you couldn't survive."

Jack turns away.

"You shouldn't be here," Jack says, to all of the apparitions – all aspects of his own mind, not a one of them representing anyone outside himself. "You shouldn't be here." This time, to himself. And it's true. He shouldn't.

"But you have work to do," the Prince of the Stable Door tells him. "You aren't alone, you've never been alone, and you *are* a fighter."

"I've never been a fighter."

"You're known," the Prince tells him. "You're a legend, among the damned and the damning, among the dark and princely. You defeated the Thorns, and you did it yourself."

"You worked through me."

The Prince of the Stable Door smiles. "I fought beside you, yes, and I gave you my strength and my skills, but it was your body, your mind and heart, your soul in that fight."

"What am I supposed to do?" Jack asks.

"What do you think?"

"Save the world?"

The Prince of the Stable Door smiles. "Do you think any one person can do that?"

"Yes?" Jack asks. Then he lowers his head. "No. No, I don't think so."

"There's a balance to be maintained," the Prince of the Stable Door says. "One person can tilt the scales."

Jack shakes his head. "I can't just fight my way through legions."

"No," the Prince of the Stable Door says. "You can't."

Light comes with consciousness. When Jack Harlow opens his eyes, he's on his back and the sun is high and blinding. He tries to sit up, but there's too much pain, so he stays down and says, "Colton?"

The warlock, however, is not beside him. It's Kalinda. She's pressing cool towels to Jack's forehead. "Your voice sounds terrible, love."

"What happened?"

"We won the night," Kalinda says. "You fought like a maniac. You scared a lot of people. On both sides."

"War is supposed to be scary," Jack says.

Kalinda shakes her head. "This isn't war, love. This is just a battle. A skirmish. This is merely the upsetting of balance. There's always a line that mustn't be crossed, and the darkness has crossed it – and they will cross it again."

"Tonight."

"Yes, tonight," Kalinda says, "but you know that's not what I meant."

"So what are we doing here?" Jack asks.

"Licking our wounds."

"How bad was it?"

"After you fell, the legion came in like a swarm. We held them back."

"Why am I still alive?"

"Hard to kill, I suspect. I watched that thing crush you, love. You shouldn't have bones anymore. Then you got up and dissolved it, every ounce of it, into some sort of liquid metal. Mercury, I would've thought, but it's actually liquid silver."

"I don't remember that."

She nods. "It's okay, you don't have to. I'm not the one who fears you."

"Jonathan Harlow."

"He knows what you are, love, and where you're from. He believes you're a threat."

"And you?"

She smiles. "I *know* you're a threat. But you haven't threatened me." She dips the towel into her bowl of ice water and pats Jack's forehead again. "How do you feel?"

"Angry."

"Why do you trust me, Jack Harlow?"

It's Jack's turn to smile. He doesn't know how well it comes across. "You're the first person in a long time not trying to make me do something."

"Oh, but I am," Kalinda says. "I want you to realize who you are, and your own potential, and I want you to bring that to bear against the kings of the mountain."

"You think I can do that?"

"I know that one person can tilt the scales of balance," Kalinda says. "The kings believe you are such a man. Your surrogate father believes you are such a man. Therefore, I would be foolish not to accept it."

Jack understands. He nods. He says, "I'm not a warrior. I can't return to the battle like that."

"The battle will come to you, regardless," Kalinda says. "Focus on your intention."

"What's my intention supposed to be, if not defend the city?"

"Leave the defense to me, love."

2.

Jonathan Harlow never visits his son. Jack lays on a cot in a square near the middle of Shangri La under a white cloth and a brilliant sun and the brightest, bluest sky he's ever seen. He didn't even know such a shade existed. He lives too much in the night, in the darkness, with an entirely different color palette.

He's not alone. Another dozen soldiers lay out in the sun. The vampire, he's told, did not survive the night, and his body has been burnt to ash before it could rise again under the control of something more sinister.

Colton, the warlock, has not been found. If he died, no one saw it, and no one's seen the body. But the warlock never returned from the battlefield, meaning either he was consumed entirely or he was taken as a prisoner. The men around him are just that: men, soldiers, mercenaries on Jonathan Harlow's payroll.

But the man himself, the so-called father, never comes.

That makes Jack angry. Everything makes Jack angry. He's not happy about that. He's trying to beat it back, the anger and hatred, but in the case of his father, it continues to resurface. Jonathan Harlow has left the battle, promising to send aid of some sort, additional weapons, and men to wield them and die. Exactly what Jack Harlow did not want him doing.

He lays there counting his bones. Seventeen broken. Three muscles torn. The pain has subsided, not because there's less of it but because he's cut off the nerve receptors. No need to feel it. He knows he can't walk. He knows he can't rise. He knows when the sun goes down, the creatures of the night will enter Shangri La and find a field of helpless victims waiting to be perused, tasted, and digested.

Jack Harlow draws on the abilities he's acquired. He'll heal faster than any of these other men, but he's not invulnerable. He never was. He'd never been more foolish. Anger got in the way of rational thought. Rather than simply destroy his father, he tried to swallow that anger and push forward. Despite all the man has done, recently and in the past, Jack had been willing to let him live.

No more.

Next time, Jack will kill him. Jonathan Harlow is the source of his anger – maybe not all of it, but enough that it keeps the flames smoldering inside, and as seen last night they ignite too easily. He never should have rushed out into the battle like that. He's gained abilities and powers and strengths, but not the skills, not training, not knowledge.

"I want to show you something," Kalinda says, the next time she stops at his cot. It's two hours later, the sun is lower, but sunset – *ukamirra* – is still hours away.

"I can't walk."

"Of course you can, love."

Jack reaches inside, lets the pain flow again – he wants to know if he does too much – and it's nearly unbearable. He grimaces, he cries out, he takes a deep breath and holds it and clenches his jaw.

"You're doing yourself no favors," Kalinda says. "If you merely slept, you'd heal faster."

"How do you know this?" Jack asks.

"Seer," she says.

"I can't see that much."

"You've had the ability for maybe two weeks, love.

I've had it all my life. Despite the beauty of youth, I'm older than I look."

"I didn't mean anything by that," Jack says.

"You're so sensitive. Now get up."

Slowly, Jack swings his legs off the side of the cot. They protest. But they hold him when he stands. The bones aren't really shattered, not even cracked anymore. Muscles ache, but some of these muscles have never been used before.

"Shocking, how fast you heal," Kalinda says. "Now come with me. There's something you need to see."

Before they walk, Jack looks around at the men in the other cots. Some sleep. Some believe it might be their last sleep, that they'll never open their eyes again. Some are ready to go back into battle. Some want to go home to mommy. All of them are justified. All of them have seen the worst of war on the worst battlefields of earth, and then they've come here. He reaches for them, into their bodies with his mind. He's not even sure he can do this. He physically drew poison from Colton's body at the Susquehanna Facility. That seems like forever ago. This time, he draws the lead, the venoms, the toxins, without contact. He draws them into a sphere, a solid chunk of metal the size of a softball.

Jack drops it.

Kalinda smiles. "You're stronger than you know."

"They shouldn't die needlessly," Jack says.

"Not all death is needless."

"Theirs would have been."

"They'll be sent back, mostly. Even healed, they'll need time to recover. How are you feeling?"

"Like every muscle burns."

Kalinda takes Jack by the hand. "It's a long walk, but I think you can handle it."

"Will we be back before *ukamirra*?"

"I will."

"You don't plan to kill me," Jack says.

She smiles. "Probably not. But we can't all survive the night. Another paradise fell last night, love, but now the kings know you're here so it will be a full onslaught. Every creature, every warrior, everything they've got."

"And you want to remove me from the playing field?" Jack asks.

"Just come."

It is a long walk. Thirty, forty minutes, each stretching tenfold because of the pain every step sends through Jack's legs. The streets of Shangri La are filled with the scents of lilacs and other flowers, tree sap, thick humidity, other forest scents. The trees are in full bloom, with white flowers or pink flowers, and from the trees monkeys watch, and tigers, and daytime shadows, different than the shades of night.

They walk through curving dirt streets lined with rocks. They go around buildings and through buildings, and at last down a stairway and outside on the side of a mountain. They're overtop a waterfall, which drops into a river far below, and across from another. A bridge leads to the dark side of the mountain Armageddon.

"There," Kalinda says. "Armageddon. That trail will guide you."

"Into the mountain?"

"No. Up the side of the mountain. The pass is secret, and well-hidden on the other end, but it will lead you to the heart of the mountain and the camp of the kings."

"You want me to kill the kings and end the war," Jack says.

"I want you to visit the kings," Kalinda says, "and if

you have to kill one or more, you'll do so. But yes, I want you to end this war."

"Why didn't you tell me this yesterday?"

"You wouldn't have known what to do."

"Do I now?"

"I hope so."

She squeezes his hand one last time, then turns to walk away.

"Will I see you again?" he asks.

"I hope so."

3.

The bridge is narrow but solid stone, as if carved from the mountain itself. Jack Harlow walks across it virtually unseen, though there's a raven flying overhead, and there's eyes in the water a hundred meters below. He walks, not like a hero, not like a man on a mission, but like a soldier returning wounded from war. The pain, especially in his ankles, throbs with every step. His vision, however, is sharp, sharper than it's ever been.

He has spent too long running, either away from who and what he was or toward some shallow vengeance. He'd even tried to run after Lisa Sparrow all the way to hell, which was misguided at best.

He should be smarter than that. He should know better. He should have been paying attention.

Midway across the bridge, the environment shifts. He's no longer walking through the pristine, flourishing Shangri La, but on the barren wasteland of the mountain Armageddon. The bridge remains strong beneath him, but the stones are dust, rubble held together by momentum and intention. The humidity of the forest and the spray of the river don't reach the mountain side of the river. The drier air makes him pause, but he's made it through worse.

A troll waits on the other side of the river. Big and ugly, his eyes drip with weariness. He forces a smile, the kind that probably inspired the Grimm Brothers to collect their tales. "There's a toll for the crossing." The weight of the mountain bears down on his voice.

"No," Jack Harlow says, "there's not, not anymore."

The troll, momentarily, doesn't seem to know how to react. Now that he sees Jack Harlow. Now that he looks into the DarkWalker's eyes. He clenches his fists with forced glee, but then reluctantly lowers them. "I don't understand."

"Your toll collecting days are over," Jack Harlow tells the troll. "By sunrise next, this bridge will be gone. Do you want my advice?"

"Advice?"

"I offer it freely," Jack Harlow says, knowing something of trolls and their bargains. "Leave. Run. Go far from this place. Because, while I don't know how it will end, it will end."

The troll hesitates. He's not exactly bright. "I've got a task."

"Find a new bridge."

The troll shakes its head. Retightens the fists. "It's more than that."

"What's the toll?" Jack asks.

"A coin."

"I haven't got any." Jack turns out his pockets to show they're empty, but they're not. There is a coin: the hobo nickel from the Brownstone, the woman's face staring up at him as the skull stares down into his hand. He shows it to the troll. "Will this do?"

The troll squints. "Too small," the troll says. "No, it must be gold."

Jack continues to hold the coin up. "Better to have this than nothing," Jack says, "and this is all I've got."

"Then you must turn back."

"You know I can't."

The troll takes a sighing breath. "Better, then, you take your silly little coin and walk away alive than end up in my belly as dinner." The troll's stomach grumbles at the word. Jack can practically see the movement of muscles under the patchy flesh.

"I wouldn't make a meal."

"Not a very big one, no," the troll admits.

"Let me pass," Jack says, stepping forward and showing his strength. "I won't ask again."

The troll, mean and ugly and nasty as it may be, is also tired. Jack doesn't know if he would've seen this ever before, but it's clear now. The troll releases his fists one last time and sighs and says, "Alright."

Jack Harlow walks forward, past the troll, hardly limping at all for those first three steps. Off the bridge, on the crooked, jagged path that climbs the mountain Armageddon, Jack looks back and says, "Seriously. Run."

The troll doesn't run. He does, however, listen. He listens and obeys, and the troll walks away from the mountain toward the valley of Shangri La. Jack watches until the troll disappears into the forest.

The path is uneven and broken, the rocks overgrown with the discarded chitinous husks of insect-like things that have crawled on the walls of this mountain. They crunch under his feet. He reaches, and ascend, treacherous, imbalanced steps that shift under his weight and threaten to thrown him off the mountain. The incline is hard, and at times a near-impossible ninety degrees. The mountain wall is steep and brittle, the switchbacks dangerous, the air thin and brisk.

Jack looks across the chasm, toward the forest surrounding Shangri La. The forest obscures much of the city, so all Jack can see are spires and watchtowers. He hears the preparations for war from both sides. He can no longer see the river below him. It might as well be a concrete floor. He notices, however, that the birds have chosen a side; ravens and hawks circle the forest, but other ravens and hawks stick close to the mountain, all of them flying as though a wall divided them.

The path eventually cuts inward, toward a truer, more usable mountain pass, and spills Jack Harlow into the camp of the first king and his army.

CHAPTER THREE

1.

The legion of the first king camps on a lower section of the mountain Armageddon. The officers have leathery tents made from the skin of their fallen enemies and propped up by their bones. Five such tents circle a raging campfire, next to which, at a bone table, the king and his top officers sit. There's stew of some sort in skull bowls. It smells rancid. There's also a tattered map, on which a dozen markers are arranged.

Around the tents, the king's army sits crouched, huddled close, in shiny bone armor, holding barbed spears. There are drums all around, makeshift things, being pounded in perfect synchronization by the wounded. Some of their "sticks" are fresh from Shangri La.

The king, seeing Jack Harlow, swipes a jagged, crooked arm across the map, clearing the markers and upsetting the bowls. He rises. His limbs have multiple knees and elbows, inconsistent with each other, so he cracks as he moves with a mechanized effect. Immediately, the officers are on their feet, and the so-called *enlisted men* have Jack surrounded. A dozen spear points hover inches from his face.

"Who dares?" the king demands. Only the officers are dressed, and only the king's clothes would not be considered rags. They're velvet, maybe, pale golds and reds that have seen more vibrant days. His head is ringed with golden spikes and bone protrusions that may once have been a crown but are now gnarled protrusions.

The king comes closer, waving aside two of the spears, to examine Jack Harlow. His stench precedes him. He stands two feet taller than Jack and his eyes are as pale as the sky over Armageddon. The king draws in a deep breath, narrows his eyes. "Are you supposed to be an emissary?"

"I've come to end this war," Jack Harlow says.

The king tilts his head and narrows his eyes. After a brief hesitation, he laughs, thoroughly and heartily, as though he's never heard anything more amusing in all of eternity. He swings his head wildly, looking above and beyond Jack. "You and what army?"

"Yours, if I need it," Jack says.

Murmuring ripples through the legion of soldiers. There are a thousand or more, and all of them have their attention riveted on Jack Harlow and their king. The spears nearest Jack tremble but do not fall aside.

"They've been fighting under you for how many eons?" Jack Harlow ask. "They've been obeying your commands and dying, *suffering* at your pleasure. Has a single one of them experienced a pleasure of their own?"

"My army," the king says, narrowing his voice, "rises from the depths of hell."

"Been there," Jack says. "I wasn't impressed."

The king takes a breath, then dismisses Jack with a simple command: "Kill him."

Jack holds up his hands. "I come unarmed," he says, showing both palms. "Don't make me destroy you."

The king turns his back to Jack and walks away without responding.

Jack sighs. He focuses on the spear tips nearest him and, like with the guns in the basement of the Brownstone, ignites the heat in their hearts. The bone is still organic, and Jack doesn't have control enough to limit the effect to merely the spears. Armor melts away. Bones inside the soldiers liquefy. They scream as though they've never been punished before. When Jack steps forward, the bones in the king's crown quiver and soften and spill.

The king whirls. He reaches for Jack, even as his exoskeletal hand dissolves. Through gritted teeth, he says, "Parlor tricks." But when he lifts Jack by the throat, the officers have their swords drawn and the king is their target.

One among them, a captain of some sort, says, "What happens to us?"

"You go back," Jack says, through the amorphous fist around his neck, "and the realm is yours. *Not his.*"

For a brief moment, the king's eyes betray fear. It runs deep, straight into the heart of him. Jack looks into that heart, that thudding chunk of flesh, and watches it putrefy and decay. The king clutches at his chest, but his Erector set bones are gelatin. He collapses.

"We can torture our *king?*" the captain asks, prodding the mass of bubbly flesh with his sword.

"No." Jack kneels and snuffs the king's life. Without looking up from the corpse, he says, "Go now."

The first king's legion flees through the crevices of Armageddon. Those too wounded to run, they kill – a mercy killing. The sound of the bone-armored army is a thunder that can be heard from here to Midnight. The people in Shangri La hear it, and so should the other armies, the other legions, and the other kings.

The captain is the last to go. He gives Jack what might be considered a smile and a salute. Jack says, "I never want to see you again."

"You never will."

As the captain makes himself scarce, a woman says, "Impressive, Jack Harlow."

2.

The Mistress to the Prince of Thorns, the dead and defeated Prince, emerges from unnatural shadows. Over the razor edges of her skin, she still wears a dress of souls, a thousand dead circling her and begging for release. They're a form of pleasure but also a prison. Jack knows this now. She's still enthralled to someone or something – perhaps an ideal, perhaps the Walled City.

She smiles. "I hoped to see you again before the end."

"The end of what?"

"Your world, of course." She smiles again, as though it was flirtatious.

"I defeated you once," Jack reminds her.

She laughs. "That? I wasn't even playing. You escaped the Walled City, but you opened up everything. That's why I'm here today, *Destroyer of Hells*. I'm here to drag you back to the wasteland you left."

"You were free," Jack says.

"Someone has to stand at the head of the Thorny Prince's armies."

Jack shakes his head. "You don't have to do this."

"Have to?" She steps closer. "Ah, but I *want* to, Jack Harlow. I want *you*, remember. I want you near to me always. I'd shed a hundred of these stupid little souls for yours."

The souls around her are in constant motion. None wants to be picked or chosen for any particular purpose. They're Lost Souls, the last of what's left of them, who wandered the realms of Hell for centuries before becoming fashion. Underneath, Jack knows, she's open sores and gaping wounds and deep slashes that exposure her insides. He can reach in, through the souls and through her razor skin, and pluck her heart like an apple.

"I only want you," she says. "I'll send my legion back to the Walled City. I'll lead them there myself, with you beside me, and we'll rebuild what you destroyed."

"I gave you that chance already."

"*Gave?*" The Mistress laughs again. "You think you were ever in power to *give* me anything?"

"You've seen what I can do."

"I can melt bones," she says. "You got the idea from me."

Maybe it's true. Jack doesn't know the extent of his strengths or talents. He only knows he feels physically weak, weaker than he should be while walking into the camps of monsters. Though he hadn't lifted a finger to do it, the little *parlor trick* he'd done to the first king's army had required effort. He's not yet ready to continue forward.

The Mistress strokes his cheek. Her razor finger slices the flesh, and he pulls away.

"So *delicate*," she says. "So *delicious.*"

"*Leave*," Jack says. It's a command. He says nothing more, because the threat is inherent in his voice. He speaks with more authority than he's ever known, with the breadth of the original DarkWalker and the Prince of the Stable Door and even the Prince of Thorns. Even the Mistress has added to his reserves. The nearness of her now ripples through his nerves like electricity.

The single word echoes through the mountain of Armageddon. Overhead, the ravens and hawks scatter, and even the clouds dissipate. But the Mistress does not back down. The Mistress shakes her head. The Mistress says, "Not this time, Destroyer of Worlds." She grabs him by the back of the head, scratching and tearing and cutting as she pulls him in for a kiss.

It's a thorough, deep, soulful kiss. Her lips and tongue are soft yet as sharp as the rest of her. She wraps her other arm around his waist and draws him closer. The souls around her body flee the touch of him, revolted by the watcher still inside him. And through the kiss, she draws him even closer, to join the dress of souls snaking around her legs and belly and breasts, over the sores and the exposed organs.

He says, or tries to say, "No." He tries to push her back and away, but the souls are in on it now, too, wrapping around him and pulling. He tries to resist, but physically doesn't have the strength. His mouth is filling with blood, and every drop weakens him.

He reaches up, sliding his hand along the razors of her breast, the needles that are her areola. She presses closer to him and devours his mouth more urgently. For Jack, there's not even a hint of pleasure, only pain, only slicing and slashing. He reaches into her chest, through a damaged ribcage, and extracts her heart.

The Mistress shoves him away. Jack holds the heart like a prize. It's bloody and dripping mucus, and it still pounds in his hand. She looks down at her chest, the hole there. The souls that had made up her dress dissipate or fly away or melt into the rock beneath her feet, leaving her naked, all her wounds bared, the abyss of her chest open and revealing the remaining organs. She looks down at where her souls had failed to protect her. She looks at the heart in Jack's hand, her heart, as it beats one last time. She works her mouth as though she wants to say something, but no sound comes out.

Jack says, though it's difficult with the fresh wounds in his mouth, "I'm sorry." Then he closes his fist around her heart.

The Mistress says, "I have a legion to avenge me." She drops to her knees. She closes her eyes. She says, "I really would have loved you."

"Just as you loved all your souls," Jack says.

3.

As the Mistress falls and exhales her final breaths, the legion under her marches on Shangri La.

4.

Colton opens his eyes. He's upside down, strung up by a rod shoved through his ankles. The pain brings him back to consciousness. The blood, already spilled, is dry and crusted along most of his body and face. His arms are tied behind him. He swings with the slightest movement, even the opening of his eyes, as there's not a hint of wind on the mountain Armageddon.

He's one of at least a dozen other such prisoners, all upside down. Some are in worse shape, missing limbs, or with huge gashes in their chests or backs. One is repeating some sort of mantra, a prayer, as though there might be a god to rescue her.

Colton cannot undo his hands, but he can do something to cut off some of the pain from his feet. He'll never walk again. He knows this, because he knows this is the day he dies. He doesn't know how or why or where. Details were never presented. He only knows this is the date. He feels it in his bones, even the broken bones, and he only wonders why he's been taken alive at all.

Then he sees the hordes of lupine and feline and porcine creatures, the hell beasts and lizards. *Fresh meat.* A vulture, perched atop the feet of another prisoner, picks at the raw meat of his ankle. The man, though hanging and swinging slightly because of the movement, is dead, though maybe not long dead.

From where he hangs, Colton sees only the side of the mountain Armageddon and the stark, rancid sky above. No hint of the Shangri La paradise. There's snarling and growling and barking and hissing, the rending of flesh, and the sound of sizzling meat, and he's thankful he can't actually see the source of most of it. The stink of fetid meat and raw wounds and blood is strong.

And from somewhere, there's singing.

It's a single voice, a female voice, deep as any baritone. The language is older than the earth. Whoever sings, her voice cuts through the other sounds and hits the bones in his ears at exactly the wrong angle. It hurts, to hear her sing, but she keeps the beasts that way and her voice is irresistible. Colton twists, trying to catch sight of its source. She's got to be there somewhere, just behind him, maybe not so far away that he can't catch her eye. He imagines she's horrid, some ghastly, ghostly thing from one of the deepest hells, a creature not unlike those he's seen under the mines of Silver Blade.

But he can't turn. The effort ignites pain in his ankles, and also in his left arm, which must be broken. His ribs, too. He can't count the number of breaks there, but it's both sides of his chest and it's up and down the row of them. Possibly all of them. Possibly every bone in his body is broken. The pain comes in waves, receding from one place only to surge somewhere else. Every breath is like inhaling fire.

With effort, Colton focuses his thoughts on spell work, magic and illusion both. He might not survive the day, but he doesn't have to die hanging by a spit on the side of this accursed mountain.

Her voice distracts him.

So he matches it. He digs deep, into his own baritone past, into the depths of something he's left untouched and unnurtured, so he pulls from his magic to make sure it works. He doesn't need to know the meaning of the words to match their tone and sounds. He starts small, light. The melody is simple, but the song itself is complex. It sounds like a mantra, but there's too much variation in the words. She's not repeating verses, but telling some sort of saga through her voice.

He raises his voice to be heard. The prisoners hear him first, and even the praying woman goes silent. Those words won't save her here. Nothing will. She must be begging for quick death. Then the creatures hear him. Beasts, all teeth and fangs and talons and claws, turn their attentions to him. He's screwing up the words but not the rhythm, so only a small percentage of the creatures listen to him instead of the Nightingale in their midst.

And that's how he thinks of her, since he doesn't know her name or her form. A name would help. With her name, he could do some work. Names have power. He's not without his tricks. He's not helpless, even now. He survived decades in the shallow city of Silver Blade; these are only a different set of creatures around him. In many ways, he's one of them.

His thoughts cause him to lose his place in the song. He retrieves it, but he's lost some of the creatures, and the Nightingale's voice is getting closer. She must be walking – no, sashaying – toward him. He closes his eyes to imagine her in a silky robe on stage, a dark Anna Moffo, but he cannot bring himself to think of the Nightingale as *La Bellissima*.

He realizes, quite suddenly, he's singing without accompaniment, and the shushed sounds of the beasts have been rising. He opens his eyes. The Nightingale stands before him, upside down, and she's nothing like he'd imagined.

His voice hitches. He misses a note. Hackles go up. Teeth are bared. He retrieves the melody, but it's uneasy now, with an audience like his so intent upon him.

She's bipedal, at least, but she's not recognizably human except in the shape of her lips. The eyes are draconian, lizard-like, bird-like. Instead of a nose, she's got three slits between her eyes. Her neck connects to her body like a frozen waterfall. Her skin is a dull, lifeless green. He can't take all of her in, especially not hanging as he is, especially not struggling to maintain the song.

She smiles. It's a strangely hypnotic expression, not beautiful at all but engaging, enrapturing, entrapping. As he sings, she reaches for him with a jagged claw and gently brushes the side of his face. The sharpness of her claw is apparent. It's cold, like a knife made of ice. She says something, she says something in that ancient, unknowable language, and flexes her wings.

Colton loses the song. It's hopeless now. He sees flecks of blood and flesh still in her teeth from her last meal, presumably one of the other prisoners. The praying woman resumes. The Nightingale reshapes her words in another language, something old but at least recognizable. It doesn't reach him. Around them, some of the animals swipe at each other. Others snarl and bark and squawk.

She tries again, this time in English, though the accent is confused and the words not well-formed. "You would play my song partner?"

Colton shakes his head. The motion generates new waves of pain. He says, "No. I would live, if I had the choice."

A clicking sound emerges from the back of her throat. She says, "I am exhaustion, and I sing no more today. My pets, if you let, devour you and my pets. Only music soothes."

With a single last measure of the song, she turns. For that briefest moment, the creatures seem to go still. As she walks away, sashays away as he'd imagined – though how she can move that body in that way, Colton does not understand – the animals around the hanging prisoners come closer.

"Sing, man," the praying woman says. "Sing, because our lives depend on it."

Colton takes a deep breath, but he does not sing. He realizes he's been given a gift, though he doubts it's true. Let the beasts feed. He's dead anyway, all of them are. Maybe the creatures will destroy themselves in the process.

They crowd closer. The noise of them, the stink of them, rises. The praying woman is crying now, begging and pleading, screaming.

The Nightingale, walking away, remains in Colton's line of vision. She strokes the heads of some of the beasts. The effect is like a pebble tossed in a still lake. The creatures respond to her. It's not the voice, or even the words. It's *her*.

Colton sings. He sings, because there's no hope in it, because the creatures are going to rend the meat from his bones no matter what he does. And if nothing else, he can at least offer the praying woman a brief glimmer of false hope. She knows it's false. He knows. The Nightingale knows. She stops, among her pets, hands on jaguar-like things beside her, and she turns her head to better listen. Colton sings as though his life depends on it, as though all their lives depend on it, when in fact nothing will avert fate.

She releases the beasts with a wave of her hooked finger.

They attack, all teeth and fangs and talons and claws. The Nightingale lowers her head in sorrow when Colton loses his voice. He's able to focus past the pain, on the music, the song, the last spell he'll ever cast. Focusing past the pain doesn't prevent it from ripping through him.

Before the end, he sees the Nightingale turn her attention elsewhere, and the many beasts around her responding to the new arrival, and briefly Colton thinks it's Jack Harlow, the DarkWalker, who had destroyed the mines of Silver Blade and will now destroy the mountain of Armageddon.

5.

Jack Harlow finds Colton's shredded corpse hanging alongside another dozen. The creatures had been thorough. But now the creatures are dead, deceased, returned to the hells from which they came. Their corpses are piled three and four high, especially concentrated around the dead prisoners and around the woman – the woman-like thing – sitting alone amid all the blood. She's wounded, too, scratched and bitten and gouged. As Jack approaches, she looks up at him. She wears a grin. It suggests she's got nothing left inside her, no sense, no sensibility, no pride. She licks her lips. They're the only vaguely human thing about her. She sings, words strung together haphazardly and without meaning.

"What did you do?" Jack asks.

She tilts her head, she glances at the warlock's corpse, and she says, "I told him truth."

"What truth?"

"About music." She shakes her head. "You know him?"

"The warlock," Jack says. "Colton. His name was Colton."

"He told me truth," she says. "Opened eyes. My *eyes.*"

"What truth?"

"My pets never love me. Hungry, so I set them on each other. I made them suffer, what they did."

"What did they do?" Jack asks.

She shakes her head. "Don't know. But I didn't like it."

"What about you?"

"Did something also I didn't like."

"What happens now?"

"I'm not easy to kill."

"Do you want to die?" Jack asks.

She looks straight at him. He can hardly read her. She's not close enough to human to comprehend. "Have persisted ten million years."

Jack nods. "I know what you mean."

"What happens now," she says, "I go to the next world."

"There's another world after hell?" Jack asks.

Shaking her head, she says, "Always another." She pushes herself to her feet. She spreads her wings. They're tattered and bloody and torn. "You like to hear song?"

Jack doesn't respond immediately. He says, "Sure."

She smiles. She smiles, and she sings, and it's the voice of a baritone nightingale, deep and rich and thoroughly feminine. She sings words from another language, another time, another place. One line, then another, then a full verse, and there's life in her lizard eyes.

There's movement in the field. Rustling. Whimpering. Slowly, the creatures, all the dead creatures, are stirring again, moving, rising, picking flesh from their teeth, and they're gathering around Jack Harlow and the nightingale. He notices too late. They're re-animated, and they're hungry.

Even the prisoners are moving again, tearing free of whatever binds them. Colton rips his feet from the rod that had been driven through them. Blood flows from the fresh wound.

As the creatures rise, as the prisoners hobble away from their hanging posts, the Nightingale's wounds mend themselves. Her color – a pale, sickening green – fades into full vibrancy. She's smiling as she sings, which should affect the sound of her words.

Jack Harlow tightens his fists. For a moment, he'd been blinded by pity. She'd seemed so small and weak and vulnerable. It was a lie. The song, he realizes, does control the animals, but this dance with death must be a regular thing. Not one seems confused.

"Don't do this," Jack Harlow says.

She smiles. It's too late. The thing is done. The creatures attack.

They attack with teeth and claws, and they attack with beaks and talons. They attack with fangs and venom. They're mutations of earthly animals, crimson jaguars and six-legged monkeys and snakes with three heads and elephants like the one that had crushed Jack Harlow on the battlefield.

He's not prepared to fight. But no one asked his opinion. And the Nightingale, the king over this legion of monsters, is beyond reach.

So Jack stands his ground. He doesn't fight back. He lets them attack. He focuses on protection, any and every sort of protection he can image. Crystalize his skin? If he can. Erect a magical shield? If that's possible. Transform into rock? Why not?

Jack Harlow can do none of these things.

The beasts, however, get close enough to rub their noses on him but don't open their mouths and don't rip into his skin and don't tear off his head. He maintains this for a minute, for two minutes, not sure exactly how he's holding them at bay. The Nightingale picks up the pace with her song. The press of creatures tighten, but they stop short of breaking his skin. Even still, it's an uncomfortable position, snouts and maws and beaks and claws all pushed against him.

The Nightingale pushes forward. The creatures, her pets, move aside to let her through. She sings loudly, her voice resonating somewhere deep inside Jack, in the marrow of his bones and the most primitive crevices of his mind. Finally, standing facing him, she looks into his eyes and ceases the song. She says, "What are you?"

"I am Jack Harlow. DarkWalker."

She tilts her head. Sniffs him. Pokes the slash in his cheek. "Taste of blood and death."

"*Leave*," Jack tells her. "Go away from this place, this mountain, this realm. Leave, and take your menagerie with you, and never come back."

"Is that threat?" she asks.

"Yes."

One of the attendant predatory birds caws as it flies off.

"Yes," Jack says again, stepping forward, "that was a threat."

"Saw you crumble at battle," she says. "Saw you crushed."

"It didn't take."

The corpse of Colton, shuffling through the creatures all this time, reaches Jack and grabs his shoulder. Behind the eyes, Colton's still in there, but there's a shroud over him. It's over all the fresh corpses, the fallen of Shangri La. They're possessed, not by a demon or a spirit or an alien, but by the animals that had consumed them. They've been trapped, not released to whatever should await them after death.

"Release them," Jack says.

"My pets?"

"My friends," Jack says. It's a big word. He knows only Colton. The others, he doesn't even recognize.

"No."

Jack goes for her throat.

She's not quick enough. His hand moves like lightning and plunges into the soft mass of skin beneath her chin. He reaches in, through flesh and blood and sinew, and grabs the thing that controls the body. Once upon a time, the Nightingale had been a singer, perhaps on a Paris stage, perhaps in Greece, perhaps in some faraway unknown realm that has long since ceased to exist. When he gets his fingers around the creature in her throat, he knows this, just as he knows this creature – which doesn't have a name in any language – has had a thousand hosts across countless millennia. He drags it out of her. Its body is rectangular in shape, with four distinct quarters, each filled with cilia. A hundred tendrils stick out the back of it and connect to various muscles, nerves, and blood vessels in the Nightingale's body. It tightens its grip on her. It holds on for its life. It, not the Nightingale herself, is the king here.

Jack tears it from her throat, ripping the tendrils. Already, it's trying to intertwine with his fingers. He cuts through it with his hand. Two halves drop to the ground. The dogs, jackals, bears, and variations thereof grab at it, biting down, tearing, fighting each other for scrap pieces of the parasite. Raptors fly in to grab their own bits. A meal is made of the mess.

The tendrils still clinging to the Nightingale's throat unravel, but the damage is done. The woman, who never before walked on this earth or any other, clutches her throat and crumbles to her knees. She looks up at Jack, looks at him with her own eyes for the first time, not just alive but clear and unclouded. The color, however, drains from her skin. She says, in her own language but in a way Jack can understand, "Thank you."

Colton also falls. So, too, do the other prisoners, and a great many of the beasts. They struggle for breath, but drown in the arid air of the mountain Armageddon. Jack kneels besides Colton and holds his hand until the warlock's senses vacate the body.

Around him, only a hundred creatures remain, mutant things that defy easy explanation or description. When Jack stands, they acknowledge him, en masse, as their new alpha.

6.

Dusk reaches the mountain Armageddon.

The stark light blanches, the barren rocky surface of the mountain cloaks itself in shadow, and on the far side of the mountain where the western horizon lies, a scarlet line stretches from one end of the world to the other. The clouds reflect the color of fresh meat. Inside the mountain, fresh steam and ash and smoke churn into the sky, as though the mountain intends to hide itself.

But no mountain can hide from those who already crawl upon its edges.

In Shangri La, the battle rages again as three kings launch an attack on the city. Jack can see the fires from the battlefield, the explosions, the trails of fire wraiths and demons. He counts the three kings there, only three though he knows four remain. He kneels, and scratches the head of one of the wolfish creatures, and whispers, "Can you protect that city?"

The wolfish thing growls.

"I know," Jack says. "You'll have to leave me alone to face one of the kings. But I've already faced three."

The wolfish thing whimpers.

"Yes," Jack says, "three kings have fallen, and four more must."

The wolfish thing howls. Its brethren, all manner of indescribable horrors, numbering one hundred perhaps, take off running. They descend the side of the mountain, and soon disappear from Jack's view, behind a bend and a dip in the mountain paths. He turns his attention upward again, where another king awaits him. They must know he's coming. Before tonight, only a single king has moved against the city.

That leaves the mountain unprotected.
Jack Harlow climbs.

7.

In the dark, the way is harder. Higher up the mountainside, the path is more narrow and more dangerous. Some of the rocks he's grabbing to keep himself steady are not stable. He hears the sounds of war. He hears the clouds circling overhead. Nighthawks fly overhead, possibly as eyes for the enemy.

Jack Harlow is weak. He's tired. His hands don't grip the stones like they should. He's suffering from exhaustion and dehydration and the wounds he'd suffered in battle the night before. He's drained by the exertions he's already made. He's sick with venom – possibly his own. He's drawing what he can from where he can – and the darkness feeds him. The mountain emboldens him. He's of the dark just as much as any of the creatures in any of the kings' armies.

But his body remains mortal, and has been broken apart and stitched back together.

He has time to think, but he doesn't. Jack Harlow was never a thinking man. He was never a man of action, either. Just a part of the shadows. Disinterested eyes. He'd manage to survive, but had never lived, and will never get the chance.

He slips and staggers as he climbs. The way gets steeper. If any wind touched this mountain, surely it would knock him loose. At the edge of his stamina, he pushes forward anyhow. He envisions only one possible end to this war.

Jack Harlow reaches the mouth of a cave. He wonders if he might sleep. It's not a big cave, maybe twenty feet deep, steep and well protected. He slides in, stumbles down to its bottom, through guano and snakeskin and cobwebs. I can just close my eyes, he thinks, for ten minutes.

Only ten minutes.

But he cannot close his eyes. He feels the thrum of the battle below, and also the beating of the mountain's heart. Slow but regular, like inhalations, the sound chills Jack's bones and raises the hairs at the nape of his neck. There will be no sleep. He rests in the darkness, but uneasiness grows within him faster than his concentrated healing can take effect. His muscles tense and he nearly hyperventilates. Years ago, when he tried to interfere with the creatures of the night, when he tried to put himself between vampires and their prey, everything seemed to work against him. Even the environment. Here, he feels compelled to move forward, to stand against the apocalypse.

He climbs from the cave. He can do nothing else.

He scales the side of the mountain, struggling against the rocks, against steam rising from cracks and fissures, against his own body.

It's midnight when he reaches the summit.

At the top of Armageddon, the night sky is completely visible. A few stars peek faintly through the thin clouds. A layer of arid mist covers the mountaintop. It's jagged and uneven. It's relatively flat but small. There's one tree in the center of it, a barren, lifeless, twisted chunk of petrified bark. Long dead ivy curls around it. In front of the tree, the seventh king, the worst of them, stands awaiting the arrival of the DarkWalker. The smoke, the mist, the darkness work to hide his features, but the man – the man-like thing – steps forward and into the starlight.

Tall, thin, he smiles with more needle-like teeth than should be able to fit in his mouth. He licks his lips. He cracks his knuckles. Needle-smile, from the Walled City of hell, says, "I hoped we would meet again."

Jack doesn't immediately respond.

"I have to say, I'm surprised. You were on a quest, a silly love quest, and you never completed it. Your lover remains somewhere other than at your side." He walks around Jack, circling, keeping his distance. "You destroyed a city in hell. You set three million, two hundred thousand and seven souls free. *Protector of Lost Souls*, I think I called you. But you left so many lost, so many broken, trapped in a realm that isn't even a realm anymore. You know, it's unsalvageable, since you introduced a sparrow into it. You made the whole place incompatible with our way of life."

"Destroyer of Hells, the Mistress called me."

"We all called you that, all the kings. All the powers and entities, when we talked about you, when we discussed your future and your potential, we called you *Destroyer of Hells*. As a reminder that not all creatures of the night are ours to command." He's completed two full circles around Jack, slowly closing the gap between them. "But the darkness is mine, *DarkWalker*. You are merely a plaything. I will put out the sun and plunge the world into eternal night, I will freeze the surface of this planet and enslave those who survive. They will build me a new palace to replace my Walled City, the Walled City you destroyed, and from there I will rule all the kingdoms of heaven and hell."

"That sounds grand," Jack says.

"There's no one and nothing to protect you now," Needle-smile says. "I will offer you this one chance to descend into the mountain, descend to the realms of hell, spend the rest of your existence in a faraway realm where perhaps your path and mine shall never cross again."

"You mean," Jack asks, "you'll let me walk away and live?"

"It is not an offer I will make again."

Jack says, "I cannot accept it."

"Then I fear we have a problem."

"Not *we*," Jack says.

Needle-smile grins. "Perhaps not."

CHAPTER FOUR

1.

The mountain Armageddon has stood since before humans walked the earth and before the age of angels. It has flourished and it has floundered, and it has always been a nexus point between worlds. While other places have always existed that allow such travel, very few portals are large and strong enough to support the movement of armies.

Histories and mythologies and legends and whispers tell of the heroes who have lost their lives on the side of Armageddon, and kings that would bring *another* final apocalypse – though as any scholar might tell you, when one world ends there's another to emerge. A thousand thousand men, djinns, seraphs, and ghosts have expelled their last breath on this mountain. Enough blood has been spilled to run through all the rivers of the earth. Wars and battles have been fought. Lovers united and divided. Over uncountable millennia, the sun has scorched its rock and its air, scoured its surface, depleted it of life and vibrancy and hope, and left only the tales of hopeless despair and endings.

In the shadow of the stone tree, Jack Harlow, DarkWalker, faces the seventh of the kings, who grins with all his needle teeth and says, "You brought this on yourself."

The battle cries of Shangri La are replaced with the thunder of four legions retreating from battle and returning to the mountain.

Jack Harlow moves. It doesn't matter what he intends to do, however. A spike thrusts out of the mountaintop and impales him. It enters at the small of his back, protrudes from his chest, and effectively locks him to the spot. The pain is immense. Something's ruptured inside, something he cannot recover from. He's going to die on top of this mountain.

"It's okay," Needle-smile says. "We'll meet again, on the other side, where I'll be torment you for eternities. This pain, what you're feeling now, isn't even a prelude to the agonies I will inflict upon you. Destroyer of Hells, I will create a new realm, a dry, cold place, where you and I can be alone for a long, long time."

Jack's vision blurs. He cannot hear anything but Needle-smile's teeth, his steps as he circles the DarkWalker, his soliloquy. "Oh, you won't always be alone. I will invite *visitors*. The kings, the kings you've defeated, will want to taste your flesh, and that can be arranged. Death is not the end, merely a transition from one place to another. I will usher you through that transition, *Destroyer of Hells*, and I will teach you a thousand words to describe the different levels of pain you'll experience." He's close enough to put a hand on Jack's shoulder. He presses softly, pushing Jack further down the spike that vibrates through the hole in his gut. "Have you nothing to say, *DarkWalker*? I will consume you, one cell at a time, and regurgitate the pieces, and reassemble you, and then I'll do it again."

Jack tries to ignore the pain, but it's impossible. It overrides everything. He can't think, he can't focus, he can't even see beyond the mountaintop. He feels the cold, and he feels the pain, and he feels the words as Needle-smile speaks. "You should have walked away, Jack Harlow. You should have left this place."

2.

The other kings arrive first. Three remain, each more hideous than the last. One is a walking patchwork of festering sores, some of which randomly erupt with pus or gas or acid. Another is a woman, or something like a woman, with pits for eyes and worms for hair and granite teeth for grinding. The third is pale and regal and insubstantial, not merely a ghost or revenant but something beyond that, something Jack can't recognize through the pain. Each comes to pay their respects, touching or stroking the DarkWalker, licking the sweat off his neck and the blood from his wound.

Then, there are the armies, three or four or seven legions – it's impossible to count, it's impossible to know, there's just an endless supply of them, each monster unique, one of a kind, things that last walked the earth in the days of the pyramids or Atlantis or dinosaurs. Monsters without reasoning, human-esque things with great intelligence and the capacity for wisdom, slaves and drones and the damned and the lost. They crowd around Jack Harlow to get a look at the almighty DarkWalker on display like a skewered pig ready for roasting. He has no idea why he isn't dead yet.

The entire time, Needle-noise keeps talking. "They're here to get a last look at a legend," he says. "You were supposed to be something, but some of them fought you on the battlefield last week."

Last *week?*

"Some of them saw you fall. Some of them laughed at your skills. You're as insubstantial as a ghost, and perhaps you *didn't* bring the sparrow into the Walled City. Perhaps you didn't destroy the hell. Your title is unearned, *Destroyer of Hells*, so I strip it from you.

You're just a rogue, an escapee, a wanderer without home, without tether, without dominion."

Eventually, the creatures blur together. Vampires, werewolves, yowies, Gorgons, zhen, adze, ghouls, dilongs, serpents, el cuero, old ones, phantoms – a parade of things Jack can barely see. Some say something to him, whispering words in forgotten languages or driving messages straight into his brain. He ignores them. The threats, the promises, the taunts, and the boasts are meaningless.

"But you are the DarkWalker, we know this, and we've defeated other DarkWalkers," Needle-smile says. "Not through strength or guile or willpower, but by sheer numbers. On this mountain, we are ten thousand strong, Jack Harlow, and you are but one."

Needle-smile leans in close when he says, "And one alone, against any endless number, will always fail."

Needle-smile sinks his teeth into the flesh of Jack's chest, each needle puncturing, so that through a hundred holes Needle-smile draws blood. Jack cannot resist, cannot pull away, cannot move with the earthy spike holding him off the ground for all to see. He does the only thing he can. He remembers who he was, who he'd always thought he was: a watcher, able to walk through the night untouched by the darkness. Repellent to the creatures of the dark. Hot to the touch. Poisonous to taste.

Needle-smile pulls away and spits out Jack's flesh. His perpetual grin is wearing thin. The pain has been become constant enough that Jack can almost ignore it. He can't move, can't struggle, but he *can* think, and he's been able to for a little while.

"No," Jack Harlow says. "I refuse your offer of eternal damnation."

Needle-smile wipes blood from his mouth with the back of his hand. "You have no choice in this, Jack Harlow."

Ten thousand creatures and entities and powers and beasts surround him. Clouds have descended in the dark to obscure all the rest of the world. There's nothing but the summit of Armageddon, Jack impaled on his spike, Needle-smile and the other kings, the soldiers that follow them, and the fossilized remnants of a tree now stone and shot through with silicone and quartz and volcanic ash a hundred thousand years old. Hanging from the stony vine around it, something already dead before the beginning of time, a single flower droops, a kind of angel's trumpet so bright an orange Armageddon cannot comprehend the color. Nearly a foot long, the petals drip with toxic nectar. The fragrance infests the air, working through the lungs of those creatures with lungs, into the skin of everything. Sweet poison drips onto the rocky surface of the mountain Armageddon.

Jack Harlow looks past the king and all his teeth, focuses all his attention on the single flower in this place where life has ceased to persist.

"Destroy it," Needle-smiles shouts.

And something does. One of the creatures rips the flower off by the stem. The ivy, however, is green. Two flowers sprout to replace it. And everything about these angel's trumpets is poisonous, so it burns into the creature's hand and seeps into its blood and transforms the creature to stone.

Jack Harlow smiles.

The angel's trumpet takes root in the new statue's grotesque hand. They shine in the moonlight. And there is moonlight now. The mists are dissipating, the smokes clearing, and stars are peering directly at the mountain Armageddon for the first time in a thousand centuries or more.

Needle-smile shoves creatures aside and rips both flowers off the stone tree. But the tree isn't petrified anymore. The wood has taken on a woody color. The vines creep. More angel's trumpets drop. Needle-smile grinds the flowers in his hands and shouts at Jack Harlow. "You can't do this! This – this is beyond you!"

Through the pain, Jack smiles. "You've underestimated me before."

The mountain trembles. The ground beneath the tree cracks. Ten thousand unimaginable monsters and three kings and all their captains of war flee. Some take to the sky, but most descend into the mountain, through the fissures and cracks and caverns, killing each other to be the first to get away. Only Needle-smile doesn't flee. He stares at Jack. Fury emanates from him in torrents. But it's impotent. The vines have already wrapped around his legs and burrowed into his skin. Poisonous flowers drip from his hands. His needle teeth fall free, one or two at a time, as he tries to speak, rotting away as a result of the flowers. Cataracts cover his eyes, and the tree itself curls one thick branch around his throat to drag him close. He screams, incoherent, incapable of forming words, but Jack understands the tone.

Soon, Needle-smile's needles are gone and his voice goes silent and he ceases to move, petrified now as the tree had been, in the shadow of a vibrant tree alive with hundreds of angel's trumpets. A river of poisonous nectar flows from the mountaintop. The spike which had impaled Jack Harlow decays, dropping him into a pool of the poison. He finally closes his eyes and expects never to open them again.

3.

The river of poisonous nectar carries Jack Harlow from the peak of the mountain Armageddon down toward the valley of Shangri La. He returns via the path he climbed. The nectar brings him halfway across the bridge.

The mountain continues to rumble. Pieces sheer off and crumble to the rivers around it. Larger chunks of the mountain fall inward.

A troll retrieves Jack's body, hoists him over his shoulder, and carries the DarkWalker to the city of Shangri La, where Kalinda greets them and pays the troll with coins from around the world and brings Jack into the temple. He's placed upon the altar, not dead but not quite alive, the nectar preserving him until they can do something to heal his wounds.

That night, nobody dies on the borders of Shangri La. No army descends from the mountain, and soon there's no mountain to descend from. It implodes, slowly, over the course of days, collapsing in on itself, burying the portals and closing off the nexus points, utterly destroying the mines and caves and caverns that might have existed there. The eastern sky reveals its sunrise, an explosion of colors accompanied by a symphony of birds and the contented roar of jungle tigers, and a field of night-blooming angel's trumpets.

EPILOGUE

JOHN URBANCIK

1.

Jack Harlow watches another sunrise. It's the tenth since he's awakened. He's healing nicely, and not at all slowly. His muscles ache and his bones may never be the same. He may never be the same.

Eulalia, still recovering from her gunshots, has joined him in Shangri La, and for a while, at least, they'll be able to live peacefully in this magical, mystical place.

"You can stay as long as you wish," Kalinda tells him. "But you and I both know that won't be forever."

2.

Naomi doesn't have access to the Brownstone in New York City, so her path to Shangri La is treacherous and long. It's ten days after the collapse of Armageddon before she gets her first view of the sun rising over paradise.

She makes her away around the city so as not to attract unwanted attention. Jack Harlow and Eulalia, the seer's servant from the shallow city of Silver Blade, lay on comfortable-looking chaise loungers.

She'd learned of Jack Harlow's whereabouts, not directly through the use of magic, but from Lance Turner after catching up to him in Westchester. He was very talkative, and very apologetic, and very understanding when she used her thin curved blades on his throat.

She approaches Jack Harlow from behind, in the early hours of dawn, wearing a wicked kind of a grin.

3.

In a fifth story apartment in Orlando, overlooking the fountain of Lake Eola, where a man named Jason has been living, a ghost wakes from a nightmare.

It isn't a gradual waking, and it isn't a typical nightmare.

She wakes breathlessly. She wakes the resident, the man living there, who doesn't want to believe in ghosts and tries to ignore her by going back to bed. She doesn't care. She's not interested. Only one man matters.

"Jack!"

She's disoriented for a moment, and trapped in this place where she died, tethered by powers unknown. She's had a dream, a dream of death, and her dreams are not mere fears made real. Her dreams are prophetic. They were when she was alive, even if she didn't know it, and they are now.

"Jack," she says again.

"Who's Jack?" The resident, Jason, rolls over and looks at her and probably believes she's not real. She's not substantial. He tries to touch her arm and confirms it.

"Jack Harlow," she says, "is going to die."

The resident doesn't respond to that. How can he?

"I have to go," the ghost says.

She drifts through the bedroom and into the living room and to the very edge of the window. Once upon a time, a ghoul had shattered the window. It's glass again. A barrier, like most the rest of the apartment, but she can't accept it. Not anymore. She's seen too much.

The ghost of Lisa Sparrow breaks free of the apartment's hold. She ruptures whatever binds restrain

her. She escapes into the whole big world to warn the
man she loves of an impossible danger that intends to
obliterate him.

COMING 2019:

DARKWALKER 5
GHOST STORIES

NOTES AND ACKNOWLEDGMENTS

Thanks to everyone who read *DarkWalker*,
enjoyed it, reviewed it, criticized it,
and threw it across the room.
I promise this will only get stranger.

Special thanks for the continued support of
Mery-et Lescher. None of these happen without you.

Thanks, also, to Brent Tiano,
to all my First Readers on all my projects;
the Five Horsemen (Mike, Mikey, Coop, Brian);
my various inspirations;
anyone who has ever taught me anything;
the ghost of Edgar Allan Poe;
and my Mom.

I have missed people. I always do. I am so sorry.

And as always: Sabine and the Rose Fairy.

ABOUT THE AUTHOR

John Urbancik was born
on a small island in the northeast
United States called Manhattan
at the dawn of a terrible and terrific decade
and grew up primarily on Long Island,
but he has lived in Florida, Virginia, and Australia.
Currently, he can be found in Madrid.

His first novel, *Sins of Blood and Stone*,
came out in 2002.

DarkWalker was originally published
in 2012 as the first of a series.
The rest of the series has remained hidden.
Until now.

John Urbancik also hosts a podcast, InkStains,
based on his writing project of the same name.

www.DarkFluidity.com

Proof

Made in the USA
Columbia, SC
11 July 2018